BILL TILGHMAN
AND THE OUTLAWS

Creative Texts Publishers products are available at special discounts for bulk purchase for sale promotions, premiums, fund-raising, and educational needs. For details, write Creative Texts Publishers, PO Box 50, Barto, PA 19504, or visit www.creativetexts.com

Bill Tilghman and the Outlaws
Screenplay by Dan Searles, Novelized by Brent Towns

Published by Creative Texts Publishers
PO Box 50
Barto, PA 1950
www.creativetexts.com

ISBN: 978-0-692-14537-1

BILL TILGHMAN
AND THE OUTLAWS

Creative Texts Publishers, LLC

Barto, PA

This one is for Sam and Jacob.

Also, a big shout out to Ryan Fowler who helped when I needed it.

—Brent

Special thanks to my lovely wife, Eydie, who puts up with me, and to my Mom and Dad, who have always been my biggest fans.

-- Dan

TABLE OF CONTENTS

ONE

It was hot. A Saturday afternoon and the sun was baking Fort Bowers, Oklahoma like a merciless furnace. But despite the heat, all along the main street townsfolk hurried over boardwalks as they went about their business. Some sought the shade of the few large Blackjack Oaks still left after the town's recent expansion, as they stood and swapped stories about their week.

Apart from Main, there were other streets in Fort Bowers, with simple names like Back Street, Front Street, First, Second, and Third Street. All were lined with houses or businesses. There were stables and the new Fort Bowers Bank.

A laden wagon rattled past the Tilghman-Masterson Saloon, drawn by a four-horse team, on its way out of town, travelling toward the distant, gray-faced mountains.

As it traversed the dusty street, it passed Woody's Mercantile and Gun and the F.J. Haberdashery.

Coming back the opposite way, young Tommy Morrow rode the sparkling new velocipede he'd picked up from Bennett's Freight

Office only the day before. After seeing the contraption in a catalogue, Tommy decided he must have it and the two-wheeled marvel had been shipped in from St. Louis.

As he wobbled past the F.J. Haberdashery, he waved to the aging gentleman who leaned his tired frame against the door jamb, weary at the pace of change before his fast-failing eyes.

'Howdy, Mr. James. Nice day.'

Tommy almost lost control of the mechanical horse, regained his balance and pedaled on.

The old man squinted through his glasses and raised his hand. 'Afternoon, Tommy. You be careful on that newfangled contraption. It looks mighty ornery if you ask me.'

'I will, Mr. James,' Tommy called back over his shoulder.

'Give me a horse any day,' the man muttered.

Frank James, one-time outlaw was now the owner of F.J. Haberdashery. It was certainly a long way from the glory days when he and his brother, Jesse, were the scourge of the west.

He snorted. 'When did I become so old?'

Just a shell of the man he'd once been, his hair was gray and disheveled, nearly white, in places the same color as his mustache His face was deeply-lined, and his now round body had begun to stoop. But, what did a man who was almost seventy expect? His eyesight was shot and if he had to hit a target with a six-gun from more than four-feet away, it had better be the side of a barn. Anything smaller and folks might be in danger of being shot by accident.

Frank fingered the clothier's measuring tape that was draped around his neck. It felt more and more like a blasted noose lately. He sighed and looked about the modernized town. What he'd give for the old days.

It was a time when he'd never felt more alive. Sure, he'd seen the horrors of war, been involved in unsavory activities, witnessed friends die violently under a hail of blazing lead, even lost his brother to a cowardly back-shooter, but he'd been alive. Not like now.

Frank was sure his headstone would read: *Here lies Frank James – Who died from boredom!*

He snorted again.

Frank was about to turn and go back inside when he heard what sounded like gunshots. The jarring noise had him reaching for a long-gone six-gun that had once sat on his right hip. He grunted his anger and then watched on as a 1912 Buick chugged past in a clatter of noise.

Frank cursed. 'Jesse, I swear the country as we knew it has gone to crap. Maybe you're better off where you are.'

With that, Frank James turned and shuffled off inside his store.

Tommy Morrow panicked when he heard the car backfire and threw himself from his velocipede in a desperate attempt to avoid being shot. It wasn't until the Buick lurched past that he realized nobody was shooting at him.

He breathed a sigh of relief, feeling a little bit foolish and looked around to see if anyone had seen him, but then his jaw dropped.

Sitting in the driver's seat was a *woman*. She was wearing a linen duster and a pair of goggles, but it was a woman just the same.

She seemed to be wrestling with the steering wheel of her vehicle in much the same way as a cowboy would a steer after roping it, preparing to put a brand on the animal.

Tommy also noted the gentleman sitting beside her, trying in vain to look calm, but his hands were suspended between himself and the wheel, prepared to grasp it should the young woman lose control.

The red machine rocketed along the main street and scattered some of the Circle L hands who'd come to town to spend their weekly pay. Their mounts started to pitch and buck, not helped by the fact that the young woman had given them a blast of the car's horn as she drove through them.

Perched in the back, high up on the seat, was a middle-aged woman with an irritated scowl on her face, holding what had once been a pink parasol. Now, however, it was a dirty-brown color, after the acquisition of much dust.

Beside her sat an older gentleman who wore a Baker Boy hat that covered his bald head. In his left hand was a cigarette holder, the cigarette itself long gone. His right hand, however, was being used to firmly grip the doorsill to steady himself as they careened along.

Tommy picked himself up and stared in the direction of the speeding car. Then he put his velocipede back on its wheels and ran a careful eye over it, looking for sign of damage.

'Might be safer to shoot that thing, young feller.'

Tommy looked across the street at three old cowboys standing on the boardwalk. They seemed to be taking great amusement from his misfortunes.

Red, Boyd, and William were part of the old breed of western men. Tough, hard men who'd been around a bit and now, like Frank James only a decade or so older, watched as the west they knew transformed into something unrecognizable.

Tommy ignored them and threw a leg back over his machine and settled into the saddle.

'Show him who's boss, son,' William called to him. 'Can't have a beast like that get the best of you. Might have to tighten the cinch a touch more so your saddle don't slip.'

Boyd and Red sniggered at the comments. William had been a bronc buster in his heyday and now, later in life, the countless falls from a pitching horse had finally caught up with him; his hunched form and his walking canes for getting around, attesting to that.

As Tommy started to ride away, the velocipede wobbled and it appeared that the young man was about to crash again. However, he regathered himself and continued down the street, the pedals making smooth circles as he worked them.

In his familiar, gravelly voice, William shouted after him, 'Ride that ornery contraption, boy! You got him!'

Red and Boyd had broad smiles on their lined faces and elbowed one another as their friend continued to shout encouragement to Tommy.

Then Red saw an elegant woman walking with purposeful steps along the boardwalk. Beside her was her eight-year-old son.

'Boyd,' he hissed.

The smiling man turned and said, 'What?'

Red nodded in the approaching woman's direction.

Boyd cursed. ' Hey, William, shut up.'

William ignored him and kept on with his boisterous outburst.

'William!'

'Shut him up,' said Red.

'I'm trying.'

'Shoot him then.'

'In case you ain't noticed, I don't have a gun.'

'Well, find one, then shoot him.'

Bill tottered around and stared at his friends. 'Who you all shooting?'

Boyd growled, 'You, Bronco Bill, you old fool. Stop that blasted yowling.'

William looked confused and then Red crooked his head along the boardwalk at the lady and her son making their way toward them.

The old horse breaker looked in their direction and then back at his friends. His eyebrows raised and under his silver mustache, his mouth made an almost perfect O.

'Well, do you think you old coots coulda told a man Miss Zoe was coming along,' he growled. 'A man standing there making a fool of hisself and his so-called friends are doing nothing. And don't call me Bill. You know I don't like it.'

Boyd and Red rolled their eyes and muttered incoherently.

Zoe Tilghman was in her early thirties, pretty, with shoulder-length, brown hair, and a pointed chin and nose. She wasn't tall by any means, and at this point in time, was ushering her son, Frankie, along the boardwalk as though they were late for an engagement.

She gave them a wry, almost humorous smile. 'Gentlemen.'

They nodded.

'Ma'am,' said Red.

Once Zoe and Frankie were past and out of earshot, William said, 'Now, that's a woman I can look up to!'

Boyd growled, 'You "look up" to most everything except snakes, gophers, and crawling drunks.'

Both Red and Boyd laughed at the old bronc buster.

William's gaze hardened. 'Oh, yeah, you two reprobates think you're looking good, eh? I can only reason you are both blind idiots.'

Suddenly, all three burst out laughing.

When Zoe and Frankie swung into the alleyway, their ears were assailed by the cries of a barker funneled along the narrow thoroughfare by the plank walls on both sides. Every now and then he would rattle his tin, interrupting his boisterous spiel.

He wore a bright-red bowler hat and was flanked on either side by two large men he used to keep the rubes under control.

Zoe stopped in front of him and paid the money required.

The barker gave her a warm smile and said, 'Thank you, ma'am. You and the boy enjoy the show.'

Frankie tugged at his mother's pale-blue dress. 'Look, Ma.'

He was pointing at a sandwich board which read:

The Battle at Elderbush Gulch.

Zoe smiled at him, at the excitement on his face. This was Frankie's first moving picture and he'd been looking forward to it for days.

Giving his hand a gentle squeeze she said, 'Come on,' and led him towards the opening in the tent.

Zoe could tell the movie had already started by the sound of the piano filtering out through the open flap, and when she entered, could see that the tent was almost full.

She searched for some spare seats for herself and Frankie. Most were taken up by women and children, , and even some unruly cowboys who were in town because it was payday.

Eventually, Zoe found two seats together and she and Frankie had to squeeze along the cramped aisle to reach them.

With Frankie seated, Zoe was about to follow suit when she noticed the cowboy sitting in the next row forward. *Pepper!*

Will Pepper was a local "cowhand" with a somewhat shady past. Word was that the sandy-headed cowboy of some fifty-five years, had crossed over to the wrong side of the law on various occasions, although nothing had been proved. What was certain, however, was his love of a drink, and his drunken rampages were stuff of legend.

More than once, her husband, Fort Bowers' town marshal, Bill Tilghman, had cause to lock the inebriated cowboy up for the night.

Zoe hesitated and glanced around for another two seats. There were none. She sighed and sat down.

The piano player's music suddenly changed to suit the grainy black and white images on the large, white screen. The Indians had started to attack the settlers, bringing forth catcalls from some of the cowboys.

Abruptly, Pepper leapt to his feet and shouted, 'Damn dirty, stinking savages!'

He wobbled a touch and turned to glare at a couple of watchers who scorned his behavior.

Behind him, Zoe had clapped her hands over her son's ears as the drunken tirade continued. She glared at his back, angry at his vulgar outburst.

'Shoot the red sonsofbitches! Plug their mangy hides!'

Finally, Zoe had heard enough. She used a straightened finger to jab him in his back to get his attention.

'Mister Pepper, could you please not curse? There are children present.'

Pepper ignored her and kept shouting.

Zoe tried again.

This time Pepper whirled about and frowned at the woman. 'What you need, Mrs. Tilghman?'

'Please, Pepper, just don't curse. There are little ears here.'

He pulled a face at her. 'Well, pardon me all to hell. You think just because your husband is the marshal you can boss me around?'

Zoe felt warmth come to her face and her right hand balled into a fist.

Pepper continued, 'You think you can tell me what to do? Well, you and your little britches can kiss my ...'

Eyes wide, Zoe let fly with a right that would have made a prizefighter proud. With a heavy whack, it landed on the drunken cowboy's chin and straightened him like a fence post. Then like a giant pine in a Montana forest, Pepper fell backwards across the next row of seats, scattering disgruntled patrons as he crashed to the floor and didn't move.

Immediately Zoe was horrified. She looked at her ringing fist and then back at the prostrate form.

'Best thing I seen all day, Mrs. Tilghman,' a man beside her growled. 'Remind me not to get on your wrong side in future.'

Frankie was wide-eyed with amazement. 'Wow! You sure showed him, Ma.'

'Quiet, Frankie,' Zoe snapped with embarrassment.

Before she realized it, the barker was at her side. 'Please ma'am, we do not tolerate such behavior.'

Her head snapped around and the man was taken aback.

'Oh, Oh, Mrs. Tilghman?'

The barker quickly gathered himself and signaled to his bouncers and then pointed at the still unconscious Pepper. They stepped forward and taking minimal care, dragged him from the tent.

Zoe said, 'I assure you, sir, I am not normally given to such . . .'

The barker held up a hand to silence her from further discomfort. 'Oh, no, no, no. Sometimes circumstances cause us to... um ... make... ahh... Please enjoy our movie.'

Zoe watched him leave and then sat down beside Frankie, mindful of the silence which had descended over the crowd.

The two bouncers dropped Pepper mercilessly onto the ground at the mouth of the alley and then turned to walk back the way they'd come. The unconscious cowboy hit the ground hard enough to raise a small puff of dust into the hot, afternoon air.

Red, Boyd, and William, now sitting on a bench seat, watched him hit the dirt. All three shook their heads.

Red ran a thorny hand through his thin, gray hair and sighed. 'Pepper is out of control again.!'

William snorted and made to rise. 'Someone is going to have to give him a swift kick.'

Boyd held him back and worked at getting his wiry frame erect. 'Boyd, don't hold me back. I'm going to do it! I'm going to teach him some manners!'

Pepper started to gather himself, waking from his knockout blow and Red said, 'Better hurry before he wakes up.'

Boyd slumped back down on the seat between his friends. '. I'd've whooped him all the way across the street for sure.'

Red and William just laughed at him.

Pepper dragged himself to his feet and swayed gently like prairie grass in a light breeze. He rubbed his tender jaw and chuckled to himself. 'Dang if that woman can't pack a wallop.'

Bleary-eyed, he looked up and down the main street until he spotted his horse outside the Powder Keg Saloon. The Powder Keg was opposite the Tilghman-Masterson establishment, further down the street from his present position.

Pepper spit in the dust at his feet and was about to walk off when a gravelly voice said, 'Man ought not to drink if he can't handle it.'

Pepper turned his head and stared at the three old men on the bench. 'One of you old-timers talking to me?'

William leaned forward on his walking stick. 'Yeah, me. Are you deaf or something? I said you ought not drink if you can't handle it. Did you hear me good that time?'

Pepper waved him away and started for his horse, his boots plotting a zig-zag pattern through the dust before he finally made it. He untied the reins, looked his horse over, then put his foot in the stirrup, but on first attempt, failed to mount and fell backwards into the dirt. Picking himself up he looked around to see the three old-timers laughing at his antics.

He cursed and tried again. This time he managed to hook a leg over the bay's saddle and pull himself up. Before the horse had moved anywhere, Pepper turned in the saddle and reached into one of his saddlebags. He rumaged around before he brought out a half-full bottle of whisky.

Pulling the cork with his teeth, he spat it onto the street. Then with a long pull, he savoured the burning liquid as it slid down his throat.

'Come on, horse. Let's outta this burg. We know when we ain't wanted.'

But Fort Bowers wasn't quite done with Pepper just yet. As the bay made its way along Main Street, young Scotty Cassidy was lying in wait, hidden beneath John Murphy's wagon, a mischevous grin on his face, and a firecracker in his hand.

The unsuspecting Pepper had the bottle to his lips when the first cracker exploded in the middle of the street. The startled cowboy pulled his older model Colt .45 six-gun from its holster.

More firecrackers, this time a string, crackled near the horse's hooves. It started to buck and pitch. Pepper lost his grip on the whiskey bottle when he was almost unseated by the frightened animal.

Regaining control of the horse just in time to see Scotty running away, Pepper realized what had happened. He cursed and emptied his six-gun at the bottle on the ground, the last bullet eventually smashing it.

His horse, however, was still skittish and bolted for the edge of town, Pepper on top, six-gun in one hand, saddlehorn in the other.

As the frightened horse thundered past the Tilghman-Masterson Saloon, the county sheriff, Bat Masterson, was standing out front and witnessed the scattering of people and animals alike.

'Slow down you ornery mule! Slow the hell down!' he heard the drunk cowboy shout as he flew past.

Two

For a Saturday afternoon the Tilghman-Masterson Saloon was unusually quiet, however, it was bound to become busier within the next hour or so.

Bill Tilghman sat at a table near the end of a long, hardwood bar with polished countertop and a brass footrail along its base.

The Fort Bowers marshal was in his early sixties, had salt'n pepper hair that matched his mustache, and a tanned and lined face. He always wore a suit and white shirt, while suspenders held up his pants.

Tilghman looked around the saloon casually, then rolled some dice on the table where he sat. He whistled along with the music coming from the saloon piano played by a bald-headed man named, of all things, Curly.

It was a lavish establishment. Both Tilghman and Masterson had spared no expense when it came to the saloon. There was wooden wall-panelling, a large mirror behind the bar, glass shelving that held rows of bottles and glasses, paintings of semi-naked women on the walls, a chandelier, wall lamps, and a hand-tooled balustrade which lined the stairs and the second-floor landing. The extravagance did not finish there. New outfits were provided monthly to the bevy of beauties who made their living as working girls, three of whom were lounging on a large sofa at the top of the stairs, talking.

Against the bar, Tilghman saw two cowboys, one a small, grizzled man named Vic, who wore two guns. The other was a larger, rough-looking man called Elias.

Behind the gleaming bar was a wiry barkeep named Benny.

A crack sounded from the back of the room which drew Tilghman's attention. His deputy, Bear Willis was walking around the billiard table with a cue in his hand, getting ready to take his next shot.

His name suited; he was a bear of a man with graying hair and beard along with a large, barrel chest.

That left the strangers. Four of them had arrived by car and by their looks, they were definitely well-to-do city slickers. They were over at a table by the front window.

One was a tall man, distinguished looking, fit. Standing beside him was a short, round, bald-headed man who wore a monocle, black high boots, and bone-coloured jodhpurs.

In his right hand was a cigarette holder which he waved around, trying to articulate something to the seated man.

Beside him stood a middle-aged woman who was frantically scratching something down on a pad that she held.

That left the pretty young lady with black hair and fine-featured face. She was ignoring the others and her gaze was drifting around the saloon.

Her eyes lingered on Tilghman momentarily and then she averted them when he stared back.

The twin doors squeaked and Tilghman shifted his gaze. When he saw who it was he cursed under his breath.

Pepper.

Still drunk, the alcoholic cow-poke started to cut a circuitous route towards the bar when Elias, the second cowboy, caught his attention and nodded towards the newcomers.

Pepper stopped and stared. He smiled and changed direction.

'Trouble,' said Tilghman to himself.

Not so, the two cowboys at the bar. They smiled at each other. It was time to have some fun.

Pepper stood unsteadily and stared at the short man. 'Where'd you get them pants? Your mamma in the circus?'

The man gave him an indignant look. 'I, sir, am a director of motion pictures.'

Pepper was taken aback briefly by the man's accent. 'I don't see no camera.'

'Indeed, sir, I tell the cameramen what to film.'

Pepper liked the sound of this and said, 'Then you should be good at telling the bartender to bring me whiskey. Not just any whiskey, mind you, but a bottle of the good stuff, because I ain't used to no rotgut.'

The tall man looked at Pepper and joined in. 'Sir, may I introduce myself. I am William Nicholas Selig, of Eagle Film Company, Nick if you like, and this is our director, Wolfgang Gulman. Once we finish our meeting here, we will be happy to have you join us.'

Gulman gave an index finger a twirl in the air and said, 'So, my good man, I direct you ... be gone.'

Pepper's six-gun seemed to leap into his hand. 'How about I direct you?'

There was movement around the table as everyone stood or moved away. Gulman stood transfixed, clearly uncomfortable to be staring down the wrong end of Pepper's Colt.

Selig moved across and held up his left hand to try and calm the situation. As he did, his coat opened just enough to reveal a small pistol in a shoulder holster.

'Gulman is only joking. Mr. uhmm... uhmm...?'

The cowboy's eyes never left Gulman. 'Name's Pepper and I direct you, Mr. Director and them circus pants, to dance.'

The Colt in Pepper's hand dropped and aimed at a spot between Gulman's feet. He squeezed the trigger, but nothing happened.

'Shiiiiit!' he cursed and thumbed the hammer back. He tried again, and the hammer fell on a spent casing. He'd forgotten to reload it. 'Damn it!'

'Pepper!'

The cowboy turned, and Vic threw him his own six-gun to help out. Due to Pepper's inebriated state, the gun was fumbled and clattered to the floorboards. He bent down and scooped it up unsteadily then turned and the weapon roared. Splinters flew from the boards between the director's feet.

Gulman threw up his hands and took an instinctive backward step. Over at the pool table, Bear seemed not to have heard the crash of the gunshot and kept about his business.

Tilghman rolled his dice across the table and sighed. Seven.

His chair made a scraping sound on the floor as it went back. The marshal came to his feet and he moved around the table.

'Pepper … man's a true idiot,' he muttered as he approached the drunken cowboy.

The Colt in Pepper's fist crashed again, and more jagged splinters flew. 'I… said… dance!'

Tilghman stopped behind the cowboy just as Gulman's boots started to tap out a tune on the floorboards. 'Put the gun away, Pepper.'

The cowboy froze. 'Just having a little fun, marshal. That's all.'

'I said holster it.'

Over at the bar, Elias swept back his coat flap and dropped his hand to his six-gun. Tilghman sensed the movement and put his hand inside his suit jacket and withdrew his own sidearm from its holster.

The Colt in Tilghman's fist, pointed at the center of Elias' face, was rock steady. 'I suggest you let that go, Elias. Unless you want another hole in your face.'

The pale-faced cowboy let the half-drawn weapon drop back into its holster.

Tilghman nodded. 'Wise man.'

Vic, on the other hand, thought that he might just be able to take Tilghman and started to ease his second six-gun from its holster. It was a mistake that could have cost him dearly.

The commotion had drawn the attention of a broad-shouldered young man with black hair from the back room. While Vic was concentrating on Tilghman, he missed seeing the newcomer emerge from the other end of the bar, closing the gap between them.

It was only after he felt the pressure of the deputy's weapon pressing against his crotch that Vic let the gun go, small beads of perspiration starting to show on his face. It was one of the newer models, an M1911. Of slimmer construction, seven-shot magazine in the butt, it fired a .45 caliber round, and was semi-automatic; all the shooter had to do was pull back the hammer once and squeeze the trigger.

The saloon doors squeaked for a second time and in walked Bat Masterson wearing a bowler hat and carrying a silver-knobbed cane in his left hand.

He was a man in his late sixties, and like Tilghman, sported a salt'n pepper mustache, was slightly balding and round in the face. However, his frame was still solid to look at.

He took in the scene before him and saw Vic's predicament. He said, 'Deputy, you pull that trigger and you sure are going to make a mess.'

The young man smiled. 'He sure won't be heading upstairs with Belle any time soon.'

'Vic, I don't believe you've met my new Deputy. You may only know him as Charles Tilghman, the marshal's oldest boy.'

'You can call me Chuck, little Mary.'

Vic just nodded.

Tilghman said, 'Keep an eye on Elias, Bat.'

Masterson studied the big cowboy. 'I'm sure our friend here would rather keep on breathing, wouldn't you?'

Elias grunted.

'Good call.'

Meanwhile, the forgotten film people breathed a collective sigh of relief. One that may have been a bit premature, as it wasn't over quite yet.

Tilghman placed the barrel of his gun against the back of Pepper's head to show he meant business. 'Last chance, Pepper.'

Pepper swallowed hard and lowered the Colt in his hand. He was about to drop it on the floor when the unexpected happened.

Suddenly, the young lady, holding up a solid-looking clipboard, lunged forward. Her pretty face was a mask of rage at the indignity that had befallen them. With a full swing the clipboard came around in a savage arc and hit Pepper full in the face with a resounding crack.

Pepper reeled back a few steps from the blow and tried to gather himself. Tilghman stepped to one side to avoid the cowboy as he staggered.

But the young lady wasn't done yet. She was good and mad and aimed to see that he paid for his abhorrent behavior.

Again, she swung the clipboard and once more the crack filled the saloon. Only this time, Pepper didn't straighten. His eyes rolled back in his head and he fell to the floor for the second time that day, out cold.

The young woman dropped the clipboard and her hands flew to her mouth as she stared down in horror. 'Oh, Lord!'

'It's all right, Miss …?

'Melody,' she managed. 'Melody Selig.'

'It's all right, Miss Melody,' Tilghman assured her. 'He had it coming.'

Tilghman then turned to Masterson. 'Bat, would you please drag Pepper and his two genius friends out of my saloon?'

A panic-stricken expression came to Elias' face. 'I ain't going to no jail!'

Elias ran for the back door of the saloon, an avenue he thought was clear. Chuck raised his M1911 and took aim at the fleeing man, then shrugged his shoulders and lowered the weapon.

The lumbering Elias' path took him past Bear who was still playing pool despite the ongoing distraction. For a big man, Bear could move quickly, a trait which many had fallen prey to over the years.

As Elias drew level with the deputy, the latter pivoted and twirled the pool cue like an expert. Coming to a stop, the thin end of the cue was in Bear's hands and he swung it like a baseball bat.

The sound of wood on bone rang out crisp and clear. The cue shattered from the force of the impact and Elias went down as though poleaxed. He didn't move.

Bear looked at the shattered cue in his hands and shook his head at the waste of a good cue. Then he tossed the splintered remains away with a clatter and walked over to the rack to get another one.

Masterson looked at Tilghman and winced. 'That hurt.'

Tilghman nodded and said, 'Always the hard way... Bat, Chuck, just hold them for a day or two. Let them cool down.'

The sheriff said, 'My pleasure, Bill.'

Tilghman put his Colt away and headed back to his table. As he neared Bear he said, 'Glad I didn't disturb your game, Deputy.'

Bear gave him a wry smile and kept playing.

Tilghman had no sooner sat down when he was approached by the city folk. They stopped in front of his table and he looked up from rolling another seven with his dice.

It was Selig who spoke. 'Excuse me. You must be Marshal Bill Tilghman? The way you handled that situation ...'

Tilghman cut him short. 'Could be. Who wants to know?'

'I'm Nick Selig, Eagle Film Company. This is our Director, Wolfgang Gulman, and our Production Supervisor, Edith Hathaway. If she doesn't like it, it's out of the film. And my daughter, Melody, who is fresh from St. Mary's Seminary.'

Tilghman's gaze settled on Melody. He raised his eyebrows and asked, 'They teach you them moves at that place?'

This brought a smile to her lips and she replied, 'Tough lunch crowd.'

'Remind me not to cut in front of you,' Tilghman said, and looked at Gulman.

His heels clicked together. 'Herr Tilghman.'

Tilghman moaned. 'Hollywood land?'

Selig nodded. 'Yes, sir.'

'California?'

'Yes, sir.'

'What do you want with me?'

'Mr. Tilghman, sir. We have a proposition for you.'

Tilghman hesitated as he watched Masterson and Chuck escorting the three cowboys out of the saloon. He looked back at Selig and said, 'You better tell me about it.'

Selig licked his lips and started. 'We want to do a movie with you in it. You and Mr. Masterson ...' He pointed at Bear. 'Even him.'

'What?' said Bear.

'That's right,' Selig confirmed. 'We want you and ... and some outlaws to go with it.'

'I'm sure you can find some folks to fill that position for you.'

Selig shook his head. 'You don't understand. We want real outlaws. Famous ones like Cole Younger. Even Frank James. We heard he was here in town.'

Tilghman shook his head. 'You're crazy, Mr. Selig.'

Selig took a piece of paper out of his pocket and wrote something on it. He pushed it across the table. 'This crazy?'

Tilghman picked the paper up and studied it. He raised his eyebrows and stared back at Selig. 'That's a whole lot of crazy right there, Mr. Selig.'

'Then let me tell you how crazy I really am.'

The sun was setting and the surrounding landscape was bathed in orange when Chuck swung the gate closed after he and his father had walked through the opening. The Tilghman house was a single-story clapboard affair, painted white like the picket fence surrounding it. Inside the fence were a variety of flowering plants that Zoe took great pride in.

They were both still laughing about the incident in the saloon, and the way that Melody had put Pepper down for the count, when the screen door banged open and young Frankie came flying out of the house and across the timber porch.

'Hey, Pa!' he shouted, and grabbed his father around the waist.

Tilghman rubbed the boy's hair and said, 'Hey, bud.'

The sheriff shifted his gaze along the porch to where another of his sons, sixteen-year-old Tench sat whittling a stick. With his dark hair he was the one who looked most like his father.

There with him was Malachi, the gunsmith's son. He too was fiddling with his knife.

'Tench, Malachi,' Tilghman greeted them.

'Hey, Pa,' Tench said, not even raising his head.

The young black boy looked up and smiled broadly. 'Hey, Mr. Tilghman. Catch many outlaws today?'

'Too many, Malachi. Too many.' It was Tilghman's standard response to Malachi's standard question.

'Daddy, did you hear what Momma did?' there was excitement in Frankie's voice.

Tilghman opened his mouth to speak when Frankie couldn't hold it back anymore. 'Daddy. Ma's been fighting again.'

'What?'

Tench said, 'Heard Ma dropped a cowpoke with one punch.'

'Shit, Tench, I was telling Pa,' grumbled Frankie.

'Watch your mouth, boy,' Tilghman cautioned the youngster.

'You say it. I heard you.'

'Well don't let your ma hear you saying it and I ain't proud of it. Just a bad habit you don't need, Son,' Tilghman said, and scooped Frankie up and carried him inside.

Tilghman found Zoe sitting at the kitchen table with her hand soaking in a bowl of cold water. He leaned down, kissed her on the forehead and said, 'Once you finish there I'll take you in for assaulting a member of the public.'

She glared at him.

The kitchen wasn't overly big and sparsely furnished. On the table in front of Zoe, sat a vase containing fresh-picked flowers. Over at the stove stood an older woman with grey hair.

'Hi, Momma,' Tilghman said.

'Bill.'

'You should've seen Ma,' Frankie interrupted. 'One punch!'

Tilghman frowned at his son. 'Go make yourself useful, boy.'

Frankie left reluctantly and once he was gone, Tilghman sat down across from his wife, a wry smile on his face.

When Zoe finally spoke, there was genuine remorse in her voice. 'Bill, I don't know what happened. You know that troublemaker, Will Pepper, he was in the flicker house. He just kept cursing and it seemed like my fist just took on a life of its own, and POW! Down he went.'

'Damn, woman, that's impressive.'

Zoe's eyebrows knitted, and she growled, 'It's not funny, Bill, and don't curse.'

Tilghman tried to look serious, but it was no use. 'Sorry, ma'am. You just gotta stop popping folks. You're getting a reputation.'

'You shut up, Bill Tilghman,' Zoe snapped. 'You're not funny.'

A time later they all sat around the table to eat the evening meal. Malachi had also joined them as he and his father quite often did.

Zoe looked across the table at the young man and asked, 'Malachi, will your Daddy be joining us this evening?'

Malachi waited until he'd finished chewing before he said, 'No, Ma'am, He's working late again.'

'One of the reasons your Pop is the best gunsmith around is he works at it,' Tilghman told Malachi.

'Yes, sir.'

'How is Woody, Malachi?' Zoe asked.

'Fine, Ma'am.'

Momma said, 'Now boys, let that be a lesson to you. Malachi, your daddy don't sit around whittling his life away or abusing trees with a pig sticker. No, he works at a respectable craft. People are proud to own a Woody Jeffries' gun because there ain't none better.'

'Now, Momma,' said Zoe. 'Malachi works at his daddy's shop most days and you know Tench is apprenticing at the livery and going to school. They can take a little time to eat dinner, right?'

'I guess so, but compared to when I was young, well, no one works like we did coming up.'

After a glance from Zoe, Tilghman said, 'Momma, let's pray before this food gets too cold to eat. Chuck, would you lead us?'

Chuck's face fell. 'Aw, Pa. You know I'm not good at giving the blessing.'

Tilghman shifted his gaze. 'How about you, Tench?'

Tench started without any hesitation. 'Thank you, Lord, for the food. And please, Lord, help Momma be more tolerant of those she don't understand.'

Zoe glared at her son. But before she could speak, Momma said, 'And Lord Jesus, help these boys tolerate this old woman who don't understand them but loves them. And who controls the food they're putting in their smart little mouths. Amen.'

Everybody laughed out loud and when things had quieted, Tilghman said, 'Good point Momma. Boys, don't mess with the cook. Right, Frankie?'

Frankie nodded his agreement. 'Right, Pop. Never mess with the cook.'

After the evening meal, Zoe stood at the kitchen sink washing the dishes when Tilghman filled the doorway and leaned against the jamb.

'Interested in drying a few dishes?' she asked jokingly. Then she frowned. 'Everything OK?'

'I had an interesting proposition today. Kind of my own flicker experience.'

Zoe wiped her hands on her apron and gave him a confused stare. 'Were you at the show? I didn't see you.'

Tilghman shook his head. 'Nope, the saloon. Some folks from Hollywoodland, want to put me on the screen.'

Zoe smiled. 'I'm not sure they've got one big enough.'

Tilghman moved into the room. 'It's true. This Hollywood fella wants Bat and Bear and me to make a picture show about outlaws. Thing is they want us. Not play actors, *us*. And, Zoe, they want the real outlaws, too. This bullgoose named Selig says people back east are clamoring for the real thing, not make believe. He knows Tom Osborne, the warden at the territorial prison. We'll be able to get a few prominent hard cases out and have them rob the bank. Then there's this big shoot-out and we lock them up. And can you believe it will take two whole weeks to make this happen?'

Concern showed on Zoe's face. 'Sounds like a good way to get yourself shot.'

Tilghman tried to allay her fears. 'No real bullets and the prisoners will always be under guard.'

'You sound as if you are considering being a party to this nonsense.'

'Zoe, it's a chance to set the record straight. The dime novels are everywhere, making those outlaws into heroes! Hell, scoundrels, murderers, and thieves is all they were, but now they are heroes. This flicker could show what the west used to be like.'

Zoe stared at him in disbelief and Tilghman knew it was time to play his trump card. He held out the piece of paper that Selig had given him.

Zoe took it and began to run a skeptical gaze over it. Her expression changed instantly, and her eyes widened. That was when Tilghman knew he had her.

She looked up at him in amazement. 'That's more money than you've made in the last five years.'

Tilghman nodded. 'Yep, and Bat and the boys will get a good payday as well.'

Zoe asked him tentatively, 'What do you think?'

'I think I'm going to say yes before they come to their senses.'

THREE

The Buick came to a stop inside the large sandstone walls of the Wild River Territorial Prison and Bear let out a long sigh of relief and grumbled, 'Last time I ever drive me one of them vehicle thingys.'

The road to the prison had been a bumpy, rutted, and winding affair which cut through timbered hills and endured two shallow, if rocky, creek crossings, before flattening out on the run in to the enormous structure.

Tilghman, Selig, and Melody had all chosen to ride horses for the journey out to the prison. Both city folk proved quite adept and capable with the four-legged beasts. They dismounted and Tilghman rolled his eyes as he watched Gulman climb from the car and swap his pith helmet for a Stetson.

'City folk,' he murmured.

Upon the high, sandstone wall, their arrival had been watched by two guards. Both men were dressed in dark-blue uniforms and carried rifles.

'What on hell's train is this?' the first guard asked.

'The Warden says he's from a little town in California called "Hollywoodland",' answered his friend.

'Remind me to stay the far, far away from that place,' the first guard growled.

'You and me both.'

Tilghman looked around the prison yard and saw at least four men he'd put there. One was a bank robber by the name of Green, another a wife-beater; Fish was his name. The other two were petty criminals who'd stepped over the line more than once.

He turned back and saw the approach of Tom Osborne, the warden, flanked by two burly guards.

He shook hands with Selig and Tilghman. He turned to Gulman and looked back at Tilghman. 'Who is he; Cody or Hickok?'

Tilghman smiled and looked at the director. He was mumbling to himself and looked a touch pale as he surveyed his surroundings. 'Looks a tad nervous, don't he?'

The three of them chuckled and Osborne turned to face the women. 'Who are these lovely ladies?'

Selig said, 'You remember my daughter.'

Osborne smiled with recognition. 'Melody? The last time I saw you, you were missing two front teeth.'

'And this is Edith Hathaway. The best Production Supervisor in Hollywood.'

Osborne gave a half bow. 'Mrs. Hathaway.'

'Oh, no, no, no. It's Miss.'

The warden apologized, 'Excuse me, Ma'am, lost my manners, too long around these miscreants. At least that's my story and I'm sticking to it.'

Miss Hathaway gave him a stern smile and nodded. 'I have that feeling at times.'

Osborne settled his gaze on Gulman and walked over to him, Selig trailing behind. 'And you are?'

'This is the film's director, Wolfgang Gulman, Tom,' Selig said.

Osborne shook his hand and said, 'Pleased to meet you, sir. If you all will come with me, I have culled our population and selected a few of our more stellar residents for you to consider.'

Osborne ushered them into the hall where the prisoners were waiting. The hall was huge, with long tables and bench seats to match. Barred windows ran along the tops of the fourteen-foot walls, close to the ceiling.

Straight away, Tilghman was having second thoughts. The warden had picked some of the worst inmates there.

Names like Murphy Jones, Arkansas Tom, Billy Sunset and Cherokee Waite. All serious killers. Then there was Cole Younger. That's when Tilghman knew it was all a bad idea.

A raucous noise erupted from the prisoners as Sunset and the others, under the watchful eye of Murphy, hazed a young, blond-headed man named John "Chicken Man" Russell.

Osborne glared at Younger and made a slashing motion across his throat. The sixty-eight year-old outlaw with an imposing frame, still had a full head of hair and a mostly brown goatee. He looked to most like a pirate, who had somehow been dropped into the Old West.He even had a pirate's mischievous glare in his eyes. He returned the warden's glare and walked over to where middle-aged Murphy Jones was seated.

Tilghman watched with curiosity and he heard the outlaw say, 'Murphy, curb your livery!'

Murphy's jaw firmed, and a defiant expression came over his face. But, instead of directing his anger at Younger, he turned it on his men. 'Get over here, you dolts.'

With scowls on their faces, Murphy's men left their prey alone and walked over to join their boss.

Once things had settled, Osborne grabbed their attention and started to explain what was happening. 'Gentlemen, Bill Tilghman and these Hollywood flicker-men are here for a reason. And it's not because they want to look at your pretty faces. They want to put eight of you fine aristocrats in a moving-picture. You will be ten feet tall on the screen and live forever.'

Selig stepped forward to explain more. 'In our moving picture, you're going to pretend to rob a bank, and Mr. Tilghman, Mr. Masterson and their deputies are going to pretend to arrest you.'

An unhappy murmur rippled through the prisoners before Younger said, 'Pardon the interruption, your honor, what do we get out of this, except the pleasure of Tilghman's sorry-assed company?'

Osborne looked at Selig. 'Nick?'

Selig said, 'We'll put the eight men we choose, up in the finest hotel in Fort Bowers. They will eat steak and drink beer at every meal, with apple pie for dessert. Every night there will be two shots of whiskey and one good cigar.'

'What's to stop us from having a fine meal and a good cigar and then beating boots out of town?'

'If any of you try to escape, the guards will be under the instruction, shoot to kill,' Osborne said matter-of-factly.

Selig said, 'For two weeks, gentlemen, you will be in high cotton.'

Tilghman stared at all of them and said, 'If you're not interested, I get it. Just step back.'

Selig rubbed his hands together. 'All right then, if you gentlemen will line up on either side of the room, we will pick our eight men.'

They all shuffled into two lines and Tilghman, along with Selig, started walking amongst them ready to choose the men they would need. Following along came Melody with her clipboard, and Warden Osborne bringing up the rear.

Tilghman stopped when they reached Cole Younger. 'Cole.'

'Tilghman, you're getting old.'

'Beats not getting old.'

Younger smiled. 'I wasted time, and now doth time waste me.'

'Still taking a shine to Shakespeare?'

Recognition suddenly registered on Selig's face and he leaned in close to Tilghman and whispered, 'Great ghosts, is that *the* Cole Younger in the flesh? He's got to be in the picture.'

Tilghman shook his head. 'No. He's too smart ... always trying for a step ahead. Guaranteed trouble.'

'People would line up to see him. As they would to see you.'

Tilghman gave Selig a questioning look.

'Every Caesar needs a Brutus,' Selig told him before he turned to Osborne. 'We'll take him.'

Standing next to Cole Younger, Russell dropped his head in a solemn gesture.

'What's wrong with him?' Selig asked.

Osborne stood next to Selig and said, 'Sad case. Kid got on the wrong side of a big shot judge and got thrown in here for stealing a couple of the judge's chickens. Received a wire the other day that the judge's wife prevailed upon her husband to reduce the young man's sentence. I hear that a pardon is coming any day now.'

Selig shook his head. 'Nobody would pay to see him.'

'He worships Cole Younger. Be lost without him. Younger threatens to hypnotize him and turn him into a chicken every time he misquotes Shakespeare.'

They moved on until they reached Murphy Jones. Once upon a time he'd been a man of good dress taste, even dapper; now, no matter how hard he tried, prison garb just didn't cut it. Since the last time Tilghman had seen him, the man had gotten grayer and his face a little more lined.

He stepped forward.

Tilghman was wary of him. Underneath all his high-class exterior was a dangerous man. 'Murphy.'

'Mr. Tilghman, I never thought I would see you after the trial.'

'I told it like it was.'

The killer's eyes flared. 'Your testimony left me to rot in this hell hole. Nothing would satisfy me more than to have you rot with me.'

'You gut shot an old man.'

'He was cheating at cards.'

'He was drunk.'

'He deserved it,' Murphy's voice carried an edge to it.

'You deserve it. That's why you're here.'

Murphy snapped, 'Tilghman, you took my freedom. I want it back.'

Tilghman stared him in the eyes and without blinking, said, 'They should have hung you.'

Murphy closed the distance between himself and the lawman, bringing a reaction from Murphy's henchmen and the guards, along with Bear.

The outlaw's brown eyes sparked. 'By the way, Bill, how is Mrs. Tilghman? Zoe, is it? Hear tell she's pleasing.'

Through clenched teeth, Tilghman said, 'Don't.'

Murphy gave Tilghman a cold smile. 'Temper, temper, Bill. Idle threats don't become a man of your stature.'

Tilghman seemed to relax. 'You're right. What's the point of empty threats?'

The punch didn't travel far but by the time it arrived, the right fist had an ample amount of power behind it and caught Murphy flush in the face.

The outlaw staggered back from the blow and was saved from falling to the hard, stone floor by the thin-built Arkansas Tom. Cherokee Waite let out a roar and the big-framed man lumbered forward. Tilghman saw him coming and his left fist snaked forward and stopped the charging man in his tracks. Then the lawman followed it up with another right which put Waite down.

While Murphy gathered himself, sandy haired Billy Sunset decided he would try to best Tilghman and started towards him, fists cocked.

It was at this time another man decided to take a hand. His name was Old Joe. As his name suggested, he was old, but also tough-looking and as hard as they come. However, his entry into the battle would not be on the side of Murphy.

He motioned to a small man who stood somewhere a shade under 5-feet, known as Big Joe; Old Joe's son.

Big Joe stepped forward and headbutted Billy Sunset, his forehead smashing flush, to spin the outlaw around. He grabbed the stunned prisoner by the arm to keep him from falling and smacked him in the mouth for good measure.

Gulman who'd been living on his nerves since coming through the large, iron gates of the prison, suddenly shouted, 'Warden, shouldn't you stop this madness?'

Osborne nodded. 'Yeah, . . . probably should.'

However, he remained still.

Big Joe passed Billy Sunset off to one of the guards, but the outlaw shook free and once again rushed towards Tilghman. Russell stuck out a well-timed boot which tripped Sunset up and he crashed to the cold, hard floor.

Murphy, now clear-headed, stood in front of Tilghman who screwed up his face and snarled, 'Don't you ever speak of my wife again.'

'My circumstance puts me at quite a disadvantage, Sheriff. Perhaps, however, fate will afford us another opportunity,' said Murphy.

'Circumstance be damned. Let's finish this here and now.'

The pair were set to go another round when Bear stepped behind Tilghman and wrapped his huge arms around his upper body. 'Bill, I think he got the point.'

The lawman's eyes blazed as he struggled against Bear's grip. 'No, I don't think he did.'

'Bill, that's enough,' Bear cautioned him.

'All right . . . All right,' Tilghman sighed. 'You can let me go.'

Bear released him and waited to see what would happen next. A voice called out, 'Once more unto the breach, dear friends, once more.'

Tilghman turned to see Cole Younger smirking at him. The marshal couldn't help but smirk back. Then he turned his attention back to Selig.

Selig walked across to Osborne and said in a low voice, 'I'm not sure if they're quite what I want.'

The warden leaned in close and whispered, 'Murphy and his henchmen have been the bane of my existence. They go or no one goes.'

Selig drew back and looked Osborne in the eyes, looking for a sign that wasn't there. He turned to face Murphy. Mr. Jones, we sure would like you and your ... ah ... friends in our picture.'

Murphy's smug gaze fell on Tilghman. 'Sir, it would be my pleasure, indeed.'

Tilghman fixed his gaze on Old Joe. 'Joe, you want to be in this moving flicker?'

The old man's eyes took on a distant look. He clutched his ever-present source of comfort, an old Bible, King James version. 'You know I saw a moving picture once with Miss Lillian Gish parading around like an angel. I think I never loved a woman more. That was down in New Orleans. That's where I saw Jesus, in New Orleans.'

'Yes or no, Joe?'

'B.T., I will be in your moving picture if my boys can be in it, too. Cause maybe if we was on the screen, it'd be like walking in heaven, like I was on a cloud somewhere with Miss Lillian Gish. Dumb, huh?'

'I don't know, Joe. Makes sense to me. Where are your boys?'

Old Joe signaled to his son who walked forward. Bill looked at the barely five-foot-tall man then back at the old outlaw. 'He's your son?'

'He is. Goes by Big Joe.'

Selig asked, 'Is there a Little Joe?'

'Well, he's with his mother. She looks after that boy.'

There was a brief conference of all concerned and the list was settled upon. It was Melody who added the last name, John Russell.

Once they were finished, Osborne turned to the prisoners. 'OK, gentlemen, they have made their decision.'

Selig stepped forward to stand beside the warden. 'I am sorry we can't take all of you, but if our picture becomes boffo box office, we will be back. Before revealing our selected cast, we are elated to announce that the celebrated Frank James has agreed to be in our photoplay.'

Behind Selig, Tilghman said in a low, concerned voice, 'You didn't tell me you had hired James. You know Cole and Frank rode together, right? That news made it to California, right?'

'Sure, it did. Their reunion will be legendary.'

Tilghman growled, 'Legendary and dangerous!'

The Buick lurched out of the prison courtyard and started the drive back to Fort Bowers with a backfire and a puff of steel-blue smoke. Bear had decided to steer the Buick this time. In the back, Gulman grabbed frantically for his pith helmet while Miss Hathaway gave Bear an acidic look.

Tilghman shook his head and Selig chuckled.

'I'd hate to be your man Bear by the time he gets back to town. Old Iron Shanks will have used her eyes to burn holes right through him.'

Behind her father Melody giggled. 'Oh, father. That's awful.'

'Awful, but true. I might add, that I would be in a perpetual state of disorganization without her.'

Tilghman looked over at the prison wagons as they were made ready. There were four guards. Two, Ross and Melton, would drive the wagons while the other two, Peters and Cooper, would ride horses.

'Looks like we're about ready to go,' Tilghman said. 'I do wish you'd reconsider about Murphy Jones and his bunch of no-goods. James and Younger, even Old Joe are easy enough to handle because they're way past their prime. But Murphy and his bunch have got at least ten years on some of us. I'm not saying that I couldn't handle them; it's just if I want to stop them from doing anything stupid. Well, years ago, I'd just lay a gun barrel up the sides of their heads. Now, at my age, I'm more likely to shoot them.'

'I don't know,' Selig said, sounding upbeat. 'You seemed to handle yourself all right in the hall.'

'All I'm saying is that you need to be careful of them. That's it.'

Five minutes later they rode out through the main gates of Wild River Territorial Prison, the wagons rattling along behind them.

The prisoners sat shackled in the wagon, bumping along, breathing fresh air, enjoying wide open spaces for the first time in a long, long time. The exception was Old Joe, who was reading his ever-present Bible, oblivious to anyone and everything around him.

Murphy broke Old Joe's train of thought.

'What do you get from that book?' Murphy asked Old Joe. 'You looking for your future? Let me tell you how it's going to end. No one gets out of this life alive.'

Old Joe looked over the top of the book he held. 'Ashes to ashes?'

Murphy said, 'We're all moving around, doing, being, then we are dirt. What difference does it make?'

'Depends. We all dig holes. Some you climb out of; some you don't.'

Old Joe continued, 'This I do know. Redemption is available to all those who seek it, Mr. Murphy.'

Murphy looked at Old Joe for what seemed like forever. 'Old man, redemption is not at all what I seek.'

In the wagon behind, Younger looked around, pleased to be free of the prison walls. '"The marriage of true minds." Ah, the turns life takes.'

Big Joe asked, 'Like being in jail one day and play acting the next?'

The outlaw said softly, 'We are pretending to be arrested for pretending to rob a bank. We all become what we pretend to be.'

Big Joe smiled, 'I'm just pretending to be free for the moment.'

Younger stared out to the rolling hills, 'I never pretended to do anything in my life.'

A few miles along the rutted trail, Selig pulled his horse in beside Tilghman's. 'So far, all is going well with our …wild bunch. You know, we could have added two more desperadoes. Then we would have our Dirty Dozen.'

Tilghman gave Selig a sidelong glance. 'If you add two more, I quit. And just call them "Outlaws" because that's what they are, nothing more and, sure as shit, nothing less.'

Selig's eyebrows raised. 'I think we've just named our movie. *Bill Tilghman and the Outlaws.*'

'You know, I probably could have got Wyatt Earp and Bass Reeves if you wanted them.'

Selig's eyes lit up. 'You could do that?'

'I think so.'

'You get them for my picture and I'll be in your debt. Imagine it. You, them, Masterson, Cole Younger, and Frank James. All in one moving picture.'

Tilghman swore, 'Still can't believe you went and got a blind, old schemer like Frank James. You court trouble, Mr. Selig. You court trouble like you've never even seen it before.'

FOUR

By the time they reached Fort Bowers, word had spread like wildfire and people were starting to turn out to catch a glimpse of the outlaws who were to stay in their town while the film was being shot.

Frank James was on the boardwalk outside his store when the prison wagons rattled past. He squinted to see the faces of those inside the barred conveyances and locked gazes with Cole Younger.

'I guess age has caught up to you, too, huh, Cole,' he murmured. 'It ain't like the old days.'

'What was that, Mr. James?' a voice beside him said.

Becky Farmer had stepped out of Miss Fanny's Dress Shop and moved to stand near Frank's shoulder. Not only was he going blind, but apparently was going deaf, too.

'Nothing, Miss Becky. Just an old man's mumblings.'

Across the street and a little further down, a large figure emerged from the gunsmith shop. He had a Winchester '94 that he'd been working on, in his large hands, and stood next to his son. Woody Jeffries looked down slightly at Malachi. 'Anyone would think the circus has come to town.'

His son ignored the remark and continued to take in the scene before him.

Then Woody saw Tilghman coming along the street behind the procession. He nodded a greeting at the marshal who eased his horse to a stop in front of where the two stood.

Woody stared up at Tilghman and asked, 'B.T., have you lost your mind?'

'Maybe,' he acknowledged and climbed down from the saddle.

'How about yes. The legendary Bill Tilghman escorting convicts into town. What's this world coming to?'

A crowd started to gather around Tilghman, congratulating him and making him feel uncomfortable. A figure pushed through the gathering and a moment later the Reverend Lowe, an older man with gray hair and glasses, stood before him.

'Well, Marshal Tilghman, this is something, indeed.'

'You're right about that, Reverend,' Tilghman said drily.

'I heard you're going to be filming, even on Sundays.'

'So they say.'

The reverend's demeanor shifted slightly. 'Everybody works for somebody. Be holding services anyway. May just be me and my maker, but I'll be spreading His word. Sorry I won't be able to spread it to the likes of these desperadoes.'

'As you wish.'

'Your wife tells me the Grange is planning a picnic to welcome Mr. Selig and his movie crew. Charity warrants that we extend our invitation to include the prisoners.'

Tilghman stared at the reverend, his expression hard. 'Picnic? Really? I hadn't heard that. More good news.'

Woody gave Tilghman a mirthless smile. 'The day just keeps on getting better, doesn't it?'

Tilghman nodded with dismay. 'Yes it does, Woody. Yes it does.'

The Buick was parked outside the Blenderhasset Hotel and had drawn a large crowd in its own right, even if they were all children who clamored to get a look at the beast.

Meanwhile, Melody and Miss Hathaway stood on the boardwalk outside, silhouetted by the large structure's rather huge, mullioned, front window. They were comparing notes when the prison wagons pulled up, and watched cautiously as the prisoners disembarked from the vehicles.

A figure pushed through the crowd and straight away the women recognized the drunk from the day before. Pepper. They watched curiously as he made for Cole Younger.

'Hey, Mr. Younger, remember me?'

There was recognition in the aging outlaw's eyes when he spoke, 'Well, well, well. The great Will Pepper. It's been a long time.'

Beside Younger, Murphy Jones paused so he could listen in on the conversation.

Pepper smiled, happy that Younger had recognized him. 'I rode with you.'

The outlaw's next words were laced with sarcasm. 'Yes, you did, for almost five full days, as I remember.'

'Now I work for Frank James.'

Younger nodded thoughtfully. 'Really, now ain't that something extra. You be sure to meet up with me next day or two and we may work together yet again.'

'Yes, sir, Mr. Younger … ahh … Cole.'

Pepper whirled away and made for the saloon, a new spring in his step.

Big Joe asked, 'Mr. Younger, what do you want with that clown?'

Younger smiled. *'Thus do I ever make my fool my purse.'*

Big Joe shook his head. He'd never get Shakespeare.

The prisoners were all eventually ushered inside the hotel under the watchful gaze of the guards and one Bill Tilghman. While this happened, the marshal saw two things that troubled him. One was the way Melody Selig had looked at the prisoner, Russell. The other was the way, Murphy Jones leered at her.

This whole crazy notion was becoming worse by the minute.

Tilghman sat at his favorite table and studied the scene before him as he rolled his dice to ease some tension. Night had descended on Fort Bowers, but the excitement remained.

The chandelier's orange light was dimmed by the thick smoke created by cigars the prisoners seemed to be devouring.

'So much for just one,' Tilghman muttered.

Selig looked at him across the table. It is their first night. The restrictions will be enforced from tomorrow.

Bat Masterson also sat at the table, and like Tilghman, was starting to have second thoughts about the whole show.

'I still think a nice, comfortable cell would have done them. Be a lot safer too.'

Tilghman agreed. 'I already told them that, Bat. But they insisted.'

Selig said, 'I assure you, gentlemen, it will all be fine.'

Both peace officers rolled their eyes and looked at each other, shaking their heads.

'He had to say it,' said Masterson.

'Yes, he did,' agreed Tilghman.

The four guards stood like armed sentinels as they covered all the exits. Curly belted out a tune on the piano with the help of Russell who'd found himself a guitar, while Waite, Sunset, and Arkansas Tom found themselves a dancing girl and were proceeding to get acquainted.

Old Joe sat quietly reading his Bible at a table he shared with Murphy. His son stood with Cole Younger at the bar. Gone were the prison uniforms and they now wore normal, everyday clothes.

There was movement at the main entrance and a woman dressed in a gaudy, yellow gown entered. Although she was a touch beyond middle-age, she still retained sufficient youthfulness to turn heads.

She had long, dark hair which fell to her shoulders, and beneath the makeup she wore, her face had staved off the lines of time well.

'Alice Thompson,' Tilghman muttered.

'Who?' asked Selig.

'Associate of Cole Younger.'

After Peters and Cooper had patted the woman down she moved further into the saloon where she laid eyes on Younger.

She crossed the room and stood before the outlaw.

'Cole.'

'Alice. Still looking good. *She's beautiful and therefore to be woo'd; She is a woman, therefore to be won.*'

'Still spouting your nonsense, I see, Cole. But, my, my, it sure sounds lovely.'

He took her gently by the elbow and guided her to the table where Murphy and Old Joe sat. 'Joe, I'd like to introduce you to Alice Thompson, the owner of Sweetwater Texas' premier social club.'

She smiled tentatively at both men and sat down.

Before things settled down again there was more movement at the door and an older woman came in. She was stout and sported a small, half-lit cigar. Still somehow against all reason, she remained strangely attractive.

She hollered, a bellow really, clear across the room, 'Old Joe, you are a site for these eyes!'

Peters, the guard, moved towards her and asked, 'You ain't carrying nothing, are you, Miss Darling?'

'Hell no. Just come to see my old man.'

She turned back toward the door and said something that Tilghman couldn't hear. But then the pitch of her voice softened, and he heard, 'Come on, Little Joe. Your Pa ain't seen you in forever.'

Tilghman's jaw dropped when he saw the figure duck to get through the doorway. Then it straightened and moved further into the room, heavy steps making the floorboards creak.

Everyone in the room stopped what they were doing and stared at the mountain of a man who'd just arrived. The man was almost seven feet tall and built thick and strong like an oak tree log.

He reached up, removed his hat, and looked about the room until his gaze settled on Old Joe. He smiled and said in a booming voice, 'Howdy, Pa.'

Murphy smiled broadly. 'This is going to be a hell of a night.'

When the sun eventually came up the following morning the prisoners were still dancing, drinking, womanizing, and generally having a fine, old time, although they had slowed some. Upstairs on the landing stood Murphy, his arm around a "dancer" who was wearing little more than black corset and knickers.

Then there was Younger and Alice. The latter had somewhat more apparel on, however, she looked slightly worse for wear. Younger on the other hand, looked quite spry in his red underwear.

Unwilling to leave the saloon while the outlaws were there, Tilghman and Masterson lounged in their chairs. Tilghman's Colt .45 sat on the table in front of him while Masterson cradled a sawn-off messenger gun.

The other outlaws and guards were scattered about the room, some cuddled up to ladies, while Old Joe sat alone, reading his Bible, Miss Darling and Little Joe having retired several hours before.

A long, orange shaft of light came in through the front window and covered the face of Cherokee Waite who lay beside an upturned chair. He stirred, cracked an eye, gasped, and then rolled over.

Tilghman looked up when the front doors opened to admit three men; Selig, Gulman, and Fort Bowers' illustrious mayor, Jonathan Grey, a diminutive man dressed in a pressed suit and bowler hat.

The three men moved to the center of the room where Selig drew everyone's attention. 'Gentlemen. Gentlemen and ladies, I do hope you have enjoyed Fort Bowers' hospitality. Mr. Gulman and I would like you to give your undivided attention to the Mayor of Fort Bowers, Mr. Jonathan Grey.'

Tilghman gave Masterson a nudge. 'Bat, wake up.'

Masterson pushed his Derby hat back on his head and looked up. 'What is ... oh, no. What's he doing here?'

'We're about to find out.'

The mayor started to speak. 'I know all you folk aren't used to many surprises, but the good folks of Fort Bowers have drummed up something special. But I need your word of honor...'

Masterson sat forward in his seat. 'Bill.'

'Oh, ... noooo. This is not good.'

It seemed like the whole town turned out for the surprise picnic. Although Tilghman and Masterson had protested vehemently against it, their list of concerns had obviously all fallen on deaf ears. Now, a few hours later, under an already hot sun, the gathering started at the edge of town in a huge grassed area littered with tall oaks, near a shallow stream. The town council had even organized a band to play on a large, circular bandstand.

In the shade of an old cottonwood, two long tables covered in red-check table cloths had been set up and womenfolk were placing dishes piled high with food all along it. A few yards away, three men stood watching a pig making lazy turns on a spit, the dripping fat from the cooking carcass sizzling in the orange flames below, causing them to flare and leap.

Children were there in abundance, either playing hopscotch or running around with wooden guns, pretending to be lawman and outlaw. Across the other side of the picnic area a few of the older boys were playing a game of baseball.

Under a tall Post Oak, a well-dressed Frank James cut a solitary figure as he watched on as best he could. He saw the town's esteemed mayor flitting from group to group attempting to maintain and possibly bolster his social standing.

Even Reverend Lowe was there helping out, moving chairs and adjusting tables. He then helped Becky carry plates across to the food tables.

Someone called out and people began gathering to watch the arrival of a flatbed wagon being used to transport the prisoners. Ross and Peters sat on the seat while Melton and Cooper followed along behind the wagon. All the guards were armed with Winchesters.

Behind the flatbed, Miss Darling and the saloon ladies ambled along, dressed in their best going-out clothes.

Further back, riding their own buckboard to avoid all the attention, was Tilghman, his wife Zoe, the two youngest boys, and Momma. And following them on horseback was Bear, Masterson, and Tilghman's oldest son, Chuck. All were carrying concealed firearms, just in case anything happened.

'What did you say?' Zoe asked her husband as their conveyance lurched over a rock on the road.

'I said I told them this was a bad idea,' Tilghman growled. 'Look at it. It's a blamed carnival.'

Zoe dropped her head to his shoulder. 'Just enjoy it, Bill. Think of it as a family picnic.'

Tilghman snorted. 'You mark my words, Zoe. This will end in trouble.'

'Oh, Bill. You worry too much.'

The "parade" came to a stop at the edge of the picnic area and the outlaws were ushered down from their transport. Tilghman drew the horse up behind them and helped Zoe and Momma to disembark.

Accompanied by Masterson, Chuck, and Bear, the Tilghman family found a place to be seated in some shade not far from the outlaws.

As it happened though, the outlaw numbers were down one. Russell had hung back after climbing down, hoping to catch a glimpse of Melody.

'Look at that, will you,' Tilghman sneered.

Zoe looked and saw members of the town council fawning over the outlaws.

Tilghman snapped, 'All this carry on is making me wish I'd never agreed to it all.'

'Just think of the money, Bill. It ain't like we couldn't use it.'

'Shit, Zoe. I'm not sure I want it all that bad.'

Shaking her head, Zoe admonished, 'Cussing, Bill.'

Tilghman shook his head. 'Shi—'

'Bill.'

Tilghman got to his feet and moved over and sat next to Masterson. Once seated, he reached into his pocket and pulled out a glass. He placed it on the table and asked, 'Where is it?'

Masterson's jacket held a full bottle of whiskey which he withdrew. Pulling the cork, he said to Tilghman, 'I remember something like this in Dodge once.'

'Me too,' Tilghman said. 'And if I remember rightly, it ended with fellers getting shot.'

Masterson poured himself a drink and nodded. 'And if *I* remember rightly, it was us who shot them.'

FIVE

Pepper, Vic, and Elias emerged from beneath some trees where they'd been drinking a jug of whiskey. Of course, they were already drunk.

As the trio walked past a table where Red, Boyd, and William were seated, Vic reached out and, without trying to conceal it, stole a chicken leg from the old cowboy's plate.

'Assholes,' muttered Red.

The chicken leg stopped before it reached Vic's lips. His stare hardened. 'What did you say, old man?'

William looked up at Vic. 'He said, pass the rolls.'

'You mocking me?' Vic sneered.

Elias gave a wry smile and said, 'Oh, I could have sworn he said assholes?'

Not to be intimidated, Boyd said, 'Well, everyone mishears him say that. Every time he says "pass the rolls" people hear assholes. Say it again, Red.'

'Assholes.'

Elias' eyes narrowed. Quizzically he murmured, 'Sounds just like assholes to me.'

William shook his head. 'Now, Red, say them both together. Slow it down a little so our intellectually challenged friends here can understand it.'

'Pass da' rolls, assssssshollllles.'

'You get it that time?' Boyd asked.

The three old timers burst out laughing. Vic, however, was not amused and took a lurching step forward, anger evident on his face.

Pepper snapped his pals back to attention, 'Come on boys, we ain't got time for this.'

Vic and Elias made to protest, but the expression on Pepper's face told them he would brook no argument. Instead they gave the old timers one last glare and followed him away.

'Yeah, I'd run too,' William growled. 'You're lucky I didn't whoop you into next week.'

Boyd and Red chuckled as the old cowboy broke out into a wracking cough.

'Yeah,' agreed Red. 'Sit down, you old coot.'

John "Chickenman" Russell sat in the shade of a large oak and strummed his guitar while he watched a local blowing on a tuba. Chickenman was trying to work out in his mind how the heck a tuba worked. Its deep, throaty bellow fascinated him so much that he never saw Melody's approach until she was standing before him.

He paused and smiled at her. 'You are powerful pretty, ma'am. The sun rises, and the sun sets, and nothing is prettier than you, my Juliet. That's Shakespeare.'

Melody giggled. 'No, it's not.'

Russell nodded resignedly. 'I know it's not. I guess I'll never be a Cole Younger.'

She gave him a warm smile. 'And my name's not Juliet. But, I do thank you for the compliment. It was sweet.'

'Making rhymes kind of helps the time pass when you're ...' he hesitated, 'in prison.'

'I imagine so, John.'

He was taken aback. 'How do you know my name?'

'It's my job.'

Russell nodded thoughtfully. He hesitated about continuing, but decided to test his luck. 'I been wondering, how'd you start doing moving pictures?'

'Since my Momma died, I've been spending my summers helping my Dad with his movie business.'

'What do you do the rest of the year?'

A squeal of delight from one of the children drew Melody's attention and, for a frightening moment, Russell thought he'd lost her. Instead she turned back and stared into his eyes. She said, with a hint of pride in her voice, 'I've been attending St. Mary's Female Seminary in Maryland.'

He couldn't hide his surprise. 'Seminary? I never met no lady preacher.'

Melody laughed again. 'Hardly. Seminary is just what they call the school. I graduated this past June, but I don't know what I want to do yet. What about you, John?'

'I'm kinda tied up at the moment.'

Melody blushed. For a fleeting second she'd forgotten about him being a prisoner. 'I'm sorry. I ...'

He stopped her before she could go any further. 'It's OK. To answer your question, nothing special, just catch up with my Momma and my brothers. Then I am hoping to get a section fertile enough to grow corn, and a woman to keep me out of trouble, someone I can hold forever.'

'That sounds pretty special to me...' there was a pause, then, 'John, how did someone like you end up in prison?'

He took a deep breath and said, 'After my father was killed fighting in the Mexican War, it fell to me to feed my mother and brothers. I couldn't get work. So, I sometimes had to steal. There was this Judge, Harwell, who raised chickens just to show at the county fair. And here we was eating cracked corn and old potatoes. One night I broke into his chicken house, grabbed one of them birds right there and dropped her in a sack. But, me and that squawking animal must have made too much noise 'cause that fat, old judge snuck up behind me and next thing I know I was behind bars. Big, bad, chicken thief.'

Melody was shocked. 'That's unfair.'

Russell shrugged.

Behind Melody, Russell saw her father approaching and nodded in that direction and she turned to watch him. When he reached them, he placed his left hand on her right arm.

'Melody, we need you to take some notes about … costumes,' he managed, not wanting it to sound suspicious. He looked at Russell. 'Excuse us.'

Selig started to lead his daughter away when Russell called after her. 'Hey, what's your name?'

Melody turned back. 'Melody, John … It's Melody.'

He watched her go and then strummed his guitar, experimented with a tune and singing, 'Melody.'

As luck would have it, when they sat down to eat, the outlaws were seated at the Tilghman table.

Tilghman's son, Chuck just happened to be sitting opposite Arkansas Tom, Billy Sunset, and Cherokee Waite. Across the table, all four swapped glares which threatened to escalate into something more at any moment.

Tilghman sat with his Colt rested on his lap in case of any trouble. Masterson, on the other hand, had him trumped with his sawn-off leaning against his seat. Beside Masterson sat Bear who was still chowing down on a chicken carcass and seemed oblivious to everything going on about him.

To Tilghman's left sat Zoe and the rest of his family.

The marshal was finishing off his meal when he felt a hand on his left shoulder. He put down his knife and looked up to see the mayor standing there.

'What can I do for you, Mayor Grey?'

'Oh nothing, Bill. I'm just checking to see that everything is going all right. It is, isn't it?'

Tilghman stared across the table at Younger. 'It's going just swimmingly, Mr. Mayor.'

'Good, good,' he seemed rather pleased with himself, chest puffed out, full of self-importance. 'They are rather well behaved. I don't see what you were worried about.'

Tilghman and Masterson glanced at each other. Slowly they lifted their weapons from the positions where they'd been out of sight and laid them on the table in front of where they sat. Tilghman said drily, 'Yes indeed, Mr. Mayor. I have no idea what I was worried about.'

Grey paled and looked from the weapons to Younger on the other side of the table. The outlaw smiled at him. 'We wouldn't dream of making trouble, Mr. Mayor.'

Speechless, Grey swallowed the lump in his throat and nodded. Then he managed, 'Yes, quite. I must keep going.'

Once he was gone, Tilghman and Masterson chuckled at the man's discomfort. Zoe dug an elbow in Tilghman's ribs and scolded, 'You two ought to be ashamed. Scaring the man like that. Put them blasted guns away.'

The two lawmen laughed out loud and placed their guns back below the table.

Tilghman smirked. 'I think the poor sod will have to go and change his drawers, Bat.'

The sheriff nodded. 'I think I smelt him from here.'

'Behave, you two,' Zoe snapped.

They both bit back their laughter under Zoe's scowl.

Abruptly, the band stopped playing and Tilghman looked over to the bandstand. Standing there was Mayor Grey and the Reverend Lowe.

A ripple of moans began to sound from the lips of surrounding picnickers. They knew what was coming. The mayor was never one to pass up a chance to make a speech. It looked like now was as good a time as any.

'Ladies and Gentlemen ...' he was cut off by catcalls from a few of the crowd, which forced him to start again. 'Ladies and Gentlemen, welcome on this historic occasion. Times have been hard for many of us here in Fort Bowers. The drought has really set a lot of us back. But, this is the start of a new era –'

A loud staccato sound erupted from under the bandstand. Thinking it was gunfire, Mayor Grey instinctively ducked, along with a few other dignitaries who'd joined him and the reverend.

Most of the crowd laughed. They'd heard the noise before. Firecrackers. Their theory was proved right when Billy's big sister dragged him kicking and screaming from beneath the stand by his ear.

As they disappeared, Boyd called out to the exasperated mayor, 'Guess that boy is a Democrat!' which brought a ripple of snickers from the crowd.

He continued, murmuring to his buddies, 'Rabbits, skunks, and politicians . . . 'never had time for any of 'em,"

Red growled, "Yes, shut the fool up before he makes my ears bleed.'

William, trying to break the tension, said, 'Stop complaining. You're both deaf. You can't hear him anyways.'

'Yeah, but I can read his lying lips.'

Their snickering was lost as Grey gathered himself while the crowd settled again after the interruption. The mayor continued. 'Now we are a town of new importance. We are a town where a moving picture will immortalize both famous and the infamous. People will come from far and wide to walk the streets that Bill Tilghman and Cole Younger trod. Today I am a proud citizen of Fort Bowers; and I am even more proud to serve you, the citizens, and to welcome our guests. Now, let's get on with the festivities.'

Frank James sat on a stump and sipped a mug of steaming hot coffee, black and bitter, just the way he liked it. It reminded him of days gone by. Waking up on a frosty morning, stirring the campfire, and boiling up a brew to warm cold bones.

But it was definitely lacking something, and Frank reached into his left coat pocket to remedy the situation.

He withdrew a small, silver flask filled with rum and added a hefty shot to the bitter liquid, before replacing it in his coat. He raised the cup to his lips and tested the brew. He nodded, just right.

A familiar voice from behind him said, 'If rum and sugar be a fault, God help the wicked!'

Frank raised his head, but didn't look back. 'The infamous Cole Younger.'

'The infamous *guest*, Cole Younger,' the outlaw corrected. He raised his own cup to toast Frank. 'Mr. Frank James.'

Frank rose from the stump and turned to face Younger. He reached back into his coat pocket and offered the outlaw his flask.

Younger held up his hand. 'No. Haven't touched a drop since Northfield. But, that was a long time ago.'

He looked Frank up and down. 'Frank James, Haberdasher. Time heals all wounds, they say.'

'Not all, Cole.'

Younger nodded. 'If not, it's the grave. I hear tell that Frank James is going to join the less fortunate among us and rob a bank.'

Frank's expression was grim. 'Just pretend Cole. Play acting. An entertainment, that's all.'

'Yep, could be very entertaining.'

Frank reached into his opposite coat pocket and took out two cigars. He passed one across to Younger who took it and bit off the end before jamming it between his teeth.

'Yes, sir,' he said, 'could be very entertaining indeed.'

'What are you up to, Cole?'

'Me, Frank? You know me.'

'Yeah, I do.'

SIX

Chuck Tilghman was still seated at the picnic table, a scowl on his face. His father had designated him to watch the three outlaws sitting across from him; Arkansas Tom, Billy Sunset, and Cherokee Waite. He'd rather be with Becky, but as his father liked to say, duty calls.

The biggest of Murphy's henchmen, Arkansas Tom had been staring at him for some time and it was wearing rather thin. Chuck decided enough was enough.

'What are you staring at, jail bird?' he growled.

Arkansas Tom gave the deputy a cold smile. 'Hear tell you're Tilghman's oldest boy. You tough like your Daddy? Or is that badge just holding you upright?'

Chuck's brother, Tench was seated beside him and touched his arm. 'Chuck, don't listen to him. He's just egging you.'

Chuck ignored him. 'What are you yapping on about, outlaw?'

A broad smile split Tom's face. 'Straight up, Junior. You get a punch. I get a punch. Flip for who goes first.'

Arkansas Tom stood up from the table and moved away from it. 'Come on, *boy*. What you waiting for?'

Chuck came slowly to his feet along with Billy Sunset and Cherokee Waite.

Tench grabbed his brother's arm. 'Chuck, don't.'

Chuck shook the hand off. He reached inside his coat and took out his M1911. He handed it to Tench. 'Take this. If they try anything, shoot them.'

Tench was about to protest, but Chuck removed his coat and forced it into his brother's hands, then turned and walked away. The guard, Melton, who was only a stone throw away, stepped forward. Chuck held up a hand to stop him.

Melton frowned, but followed at a distance.

They all moved out of sight behind a couple of large Pole Oaks. Once there, Tench tried to head the trouble off one final time. 'You, sir, should apologize right now. I mean it. For your own protection, I suggest you apologize now.'

'Shut up, kid,' Arkansas Tom sneered. 'This is between me and him.'

Melton moved forward again and once more Chuck waved him away.

Tom looked at him and said, 'Relax. This is just clean fun.'

Chuck readied himself and his gaze turned to granite. 'You gonna talk me to death or tighten up your britches and fight?'

'Why, you arrogant, little rooster,' Tom snarled and stepped in close.

The punch didn't travel far, but had a lot of force behind it. Knuckles cracked against Chuck's jaw and blood flowed freely from his mouth.

Unmoved, he smiled at the bigger man, his teeth already pink with the blood. 'Shit, is that all you got?'

Chuck's right hand streaked forward and mashed Arkansas Tom's lips back against his teeth. A left smacked into the bigger man's cheek and bruised it right away.

Arkansas Tom backed up, gathered himself and nodded. 'If that's the way you want it.'

The two stood, toe to toe, trading blows that rocked each man to his boots. However, neither would go down.

Meanwhile, another observer sat beneath a tree not far away and knew that this fight was going to be something else.

There was movement beside him and Masterson looked up to see Younger and Frank James standing there, both with cigars. Younger's, however, wasn't lit.

Masterson nodded. 'Gentlemen.'

Frank reached into his pocket and brought out a cigar. He offered it to Masterson. 'Could I interest you in a Cuban cigar, Bat?'

Instead of taking it, Masterson motioned towards the fight. 'You fellas next?'

His words were met with silence.

'Lost your nerve?'

Younger seemed to take offence at his words. 'Though I look old, I am still strong and lusty.'

Masterson smiled knowingly. 'Ah, Shakespeare. But don't you mean rusty?'

'Humph. Still as I grow older, I take no pleasure in unnecessary violence. I don't find it productive.'

Frank said, 'I concur, gentlemen. No point to it.'

Masterson said, 'Then I will have a cigar, if you will join me in a drink.'

'And what are we drinking to, Mr. Masterson?' Younger asked.

'To a long, peaceful life.'

Frank nodded. 'Well, sir, I will drink to that.'

Masterson stared at them. 'Been thinking, you two seem ... mellowed ... um ... So, how did you two bright souls crawl into so many dark holes? You're intelligent leaders of men, but you've been down so many bad roads ...'

Younger ignored the question at first. He leaned against a barrel and stared at the progression of the fight.

But, Frank's eyes grew cold as he remembered why it was and they locked onto Masterson's. 'Maybe two young men are riding back to Kansas after the States War. These fellas served with honor, but their side lost. They get home, the new government has given their farm to a Yank. But, it's OK cause the carpet bagger offers them a job *on* ...'

Frank paused as he bit back his anger. 'On their own farm, slopping hogs.'

It was Younger's turn now and he, too, stared at Masterson with granite-filled eyes. 'In town, same thing. Sweep my floors, Reb. Wash the spittoon, Reb. Hell, couldn't vote, couldn't even preach at a church.'

Masterson smiled. 'I ain't never figured you for a preacher, Cole.'

Frank and Younger swapped glances before the latter said, 'That's not the point, Masterson. It's not that I wanted to... it was that I couldn't.'

Frank joined in. 'Maybe fellas like that could think that the bankers holding those carpet bagger's money deserved to be robbed.'

'Just for example now,' Younger added.

Masterson and Frank gave the outlaw a questioning look.

He continued, 'You are just speaking metaphorically, right, Frank? You aren't saying we were robbing anything.'

Frank said, 'Still if some of those land robbers and bankers where to have taken a bullet ...'

'For example.'

Masterson frowned. 'What are you, his lawyer?'

'Who could say who was really the bad guy?' Frank went on. He looked at Younger. 'For example. Jesse and I were just two young intruders trying to take back what was ours.'

Masterson held his flask in the air. 'To your health, gentlemen. Shall all our dark holes be filled with light. Yep, to that I will drink.'

Frank shook his head. 'You know, Bat, I think I'm going to skip that drink. I need some darkness with my light.'

'You see, Bat, we are just more comfortable living with our shadows than you are,' Younger said.

Masterson drew his flask back, withdrawing his offer. 'Well, hell, I'll drink to that then.'

Then, in silence, the three of them turned their attention back to the fight.

As the altercation between Chuck and Arkansas Tom progressed, the crowd surrounding them grew. Each time Chuck landed a solid blow to the outlaw, the crowd would cheer and shout encouragement. If Arkansas Tom did, the only ones cheering seemed to be his jailhouse friends or Pepper and his cronies.

Chuck ducked under a booming right and came up with his own right fist that ripped into the outlaw's torso just below his ribcage.

Air whooshed from Arkansas Tom's lungs and he was forced to back away.

When Tilghman's son followed him, Arkansas Tom swung a left that hit him just below his bloody nose and stopped him in his tracks. Then he threw a right which landed just above the left ear and forced Chuck backward.

Chuck blew heavily and spat blood on the grass. Arkansas Tom closed the distance between them and Chuck cocked his fists, ready for more. There was no way he wasn't going to be the last man standing.

Becky hurried towards the rise where she'd seen Chuck and the outlaws disappear a while before. Her blue dress seemed to catch the sun as she walked, giving it a luminosity of sorts.

When she topped the mound, she saw the crowd below, circled around the two combatants. She frowned and then a horrified expression came over her face as she realized that one of them was Chuck.

'Good Lord,' she gasped and hurried down towards the fight.

Becky caught sight of Bat Masterson under one of the trees. She changed track and rushed up to him. 'Bat, you must stop this, immediately!'

Masterson smiled, but didn't divert his gaze from the fight. 'Why? Your beau is holding his own against that gorilla.'

Becky rammed her fists into her hips and scowled at him. 'Do you men ever grow up?'

Masterson waved his flask in the air. 'If you're lucky, just before the coffin closes.'

Becky looked bewildered and switched her gaze to Frank and Younger. 'What about you two?'

Both addressed men looked at her and held their hands up in a defensive pose. Becky stomped her foot and whirled around. She grabbed her dress in both hands and strode purposefully down the slope into the crowd.

Becky pushed her way through to the front just in time to see Chuck land a left to Arkansas Tom's jaw. With unbridled indignance, she shouted, 'Chuck Tilghman!'

Chuck turned his head to look at Becky, blood streaming from numerous cuts. All Becky succeeded in doing, however, was distracting Chuck long enough for Arkansas Tom to plant a right cross flush on Chuck's jaw.

He staggered, and Becky moved forward to block Arkansas Tom's advance. 'Get off him, you no good ... convict!'

He pushed her aside and Cherokee Waite picked her up, swung her around, and forced her back into the crowd. 'This ain't no place for you, missy. Be gone.'

At that moment a tall, thin man stepped forward, grasped Waite by the shoulder, spun him around, and planted a solid blow on his jaw.

And so, what became known as The Battle of Fort Bowers began.

SEVEN

'What do you think's going on over the hill?' Zoe asked Tilghman when she noticed more and more people headed that way.

Tilghman frowned. He caught sight of Bear walking in the same direction as the others and hurried to catch up with the deputy.

'Bear, what's happening?'

The big man turned to look at Tilghman. 'Fight. Your son is involved so they say.'

Tilghman cursed loudly. 'You've got to be kidding!'

'Oh, Bill,' Zoe said forlornly after overhearing the conversation.

He started to follow Bear when Frankie stepped forward.

'Hold it, young man,' Zoe snapped.

Tilghman looked at his son. 'You stay right here.'

Zoe looked at her husband. 'Bill, you be careful.'

'I always am.'

Frankie watched until his father crested the hill and broke into a run to follow. There was no way he was going to miss this, he thought to himself.

'Frankie! Come back!' Zoe called after him.

Momma moved to stand beside Zoe. 'You stay put, dear. I will go get him.'

Zoe ran a hand through her hair as a feeling of dread washed over her; that things were about to get so much worse.

When Tilghman crested the hill, he was astonished by what he saw before him. Multiple fights had broken out within the circle of onlookers. He could see Chuck in the thick of it, bloodied and battered, but still going hard at Arkansas Tom.

For a moment, a surge of pride flowed through Tilghman as he watched his boy take on the bigger man.

However, that disappeared when he saw Selig and Gulman down there trying to stop the brawl before it escalated even more. He could hear the German director shouting, '*Stoppen! Aufhören zu kämpfen!*'

He guessed it was his native language, but what was being said, he had no idea. When he finally reached the crowd, Selig saw him and a relieved look washed over his face.

'Tilghman, thank God. You have to stop this.'

Tilghman shot him a grim look and pushed through the crowd, with Selig following. Once on the other side Tilghman hurried across to Chuck and took him by the belt and collar. He swung his son around and let him go.

'Break it up, boys. Chuck, I expect more from you,' he barked.

He turned to face Arkansas Tom just in time to catch the outlaw's clenched fist across his jaw.

Tilghman was stunned and staggered back, sitting down hard when his knees buckled.

From nowhere, Billy Sunset appeared and cocked his leg, ready to kick Tilghman in the side of his head.

Tilghman sensed the impending trouble more than he saw it and rolled to the side in time to dodge the savage blow.

Seeing his boss was in trouble, Bear moved fast for a big man, and with a huge, right fist, clubbed Billy to the ground with a stunning blow. The outlaw tried to rise, but Bear was waiting and after another right, it was nap time.

Seeing their father in trouble, Tench and Frankie came to his aid. Tench closed on Arkansas Tom and started swinging with all his might. Frankie meantime, ran in close and kicked him hard in the shin. With a howl of pain, Arkansas Tom cuffed Tench up the side of his head and sent him reeling. Frankie, he shoved away into the crowd. Momma hurriedly grabbed the young boy by the arm and dragged him backwards.

Annoyed with the interruption, Arkansas Tom turned back to find Tilghman and finish him off. He found him all right. Or rather his jaw found Tilghman's fist, for the marshal was back on his feet, bleeding, and fighting mad.

The blow was a solid one and Arkansas Tom flailed about and disappeared into the cheering crowd.

Cherokee Waite saw his chance while Tilghman wasn't looking and took a step forward. He was stopped by a tap on his shoulder and turned to see Selig standing there.

Before Waite is even ready, Selig has cocked his fists, shuffled his feet and landed two straight, left jabs to the outlaw's chin that rocked him backwards.

Selig smiled smartly and dabbed Waite on the nose with a right. 'Princeton, Class of '68, old boy.'

Cherokee Waite wiped at his bleeding nose with the back of his hand. He looked down at the smear of blood and then back at the prancing producer. His face grew dark and a growl emanated from deep within his throat.

He charged at Selig without warning, taking him by surprise. All air was forced from the producer's lungs when Waite's shoulder hit him in the stomach. They both crashed to the grass in an untidy heap.

Cherokee Waite was quick to his feet and stood over the stunned Selig. He gave the producer a mirthless smile and said, 'Foothills of Kentucky, 1873. Class of Whoop Ass, old boy.'

Selig coughed and then groaned, 'Point taken.'

The producer lurched to his feet only to be scooped up in a crushing bear hug by his opponent's arms.

Selig's head snapped forward and caught Waite across the forehead. Stumbling back a couple of steps, he let go of Selig, and then set himself to go again.

Selig held up both hands in resignation. 'Whoa, whoa. What say we quit this recreation and have a beer?'

Waite thought about the offer and looked about. He saw Masterson, along with Younger and Frank James in the shade of a large oak. The sheriff held up his flask in a salute.

Waite nodded. 'Yeah. Follow me, professor.'

When the two of them reached Masterson, Waite took the flask and offered it to Selig.

Selig smiled and took it. Without warning, Waite's right fist streaked forward and crisply smacked the producer on the chin. Selig sat down hard, a bemused expression on his face.

'Nice fight, college boy,' Waite said, a broad grin on his face.

However, Waite's underhanded move never went unnoticed. Tilghman had seen it take place. With his jaw set firm, he approached the prisoner.

Masterson saw him coming. 'Well now. here comes trouble.'

Waite turned and saw Tilghman advancing.

Younger took the cigar from his mouth and offered Waite some advice. 'Watch his left, Cherokee. He's gotta mean left.'

As Waite braced himself and raised his fists, Tilghman walked past him and stopped in front of Frank.

'May I?' he asked, and relieved him of the cup in his hand.

Tilghman turned back to Waite and offered him the cup.

Waite looked skeptical at first, uncertain. But eventually, he reached out and took the mug. He looked at its contents and frowned, put it up to his nose and sniffed.

When he smelled the aroma of the liquor it had been laced with, he smiled and held it up and said, 'Thanks, friend.'

Waite put it to his lips at the same time as Tilghman's left fist crashed into his jaw. The outlaw went down as though poleaxed.

The marshal stared down at Waite and growled, 'Friend, my ass.'

Younger chuckled. 'Damn it, Cherokee. I told you to watch his left.'

A rousing yell sounded and Tilghman turned to face the crowd which had erupted into its own form of fisticuffs. The marshal shook his head and growled, 'Let's have a picnic they said … It'll be fun, they said …'

He stared hard at the grinning Masterson. 'Come on, Bat. Get off your ass. Time for some old-fashioned, law enforcement.'

'Man could get hurt in there, Bill,' Masterson pointed out.

'Yeah, well it ain't going to be me.'

Just then another figure caught his eye. Woody Jeffries. Tilghman saw the questioning look on his face and he nodded.

Woody returned the nod and walked towards his wagon which was parked nearby.

He briefly rummaged around in the back and withdrew an old Winchester. He cast a glance back over his shoulder at the mayhem and shook his head. Rummaged some more and came back up with a cut-down shotgun.

A smile split Woody's face and he nodded. He leaned back over the side and fossicked through a burlap sack until he found what he wanted. He held up two shotgun shells and was content with that.

The large, muscular, black gunsmith broke the shotgun open, loaded the shells, and snapped the breech closed. He patted the weapon and turned towards the crowd. 'This should be good,' he mumbled to no one in particular.

Murphy Jones sat playing cards with Old Joe and Little Joe whilst the shenanigans over the hill escalated. Zoe was seated a couple of tables away debating whether to join her husband or remain where she was.

Her gaze drifted across to where the outlaws were sitting and she heard Old Joe say, 'You sure put the Jesse James on me.'

Murphy's gaze hardened. 'What do you mean by that?'

Old Joe held his stare. 'Don't mean nothing.'

'Words can be dangerous.'

But Old Joe wouldn't be intimidated. He was still looking at Murphy when he spoke. 'Little Joe, where is your brother?'

'Dancing.'

Old Joe looked to where his son was pointing. Sure enough, there he was, in the arms of one of the local women, head placed strategically between her ample breasts, moving slowly to the music.

Old Joe chuckled. 'Well, he always had a way with the ladies.'

Another hand was dealt, and Murphy scooped up his cards. He examined them and then slammed them down on top of the table, his face a mask of disgust. Then he rose from the seat and was about to walk away when he spotted Zoe Tilghman.

He walked over to her, removed his hat, and dropped it on the table. Then he sat beside her.

Zoe's face screwed up, the man's closeness nauseated her.

He gave her a menacing smile. 'Well, Mrs. Tilghman, it seems we are alone.'

The outlaw placed his hand on her leg and Zoe tried to move away, only for Murphy to tighten his grip hard enough to make her wince.

She stared at him and hissed through gritted teeth, 'Bill would kill you for this.'

Murphy laughed out loud. 'You are all lopsided in your thoughts, Mrs. Tilghman. The fun is in goading him to try.'

A voice said, 'Murphy, I would consider it a favor between you and me if you just back off.'

Murphy gave Old Joe a cursory glance and ignored him.

Old Joe glanced at his son and Little Joe rose from his seat, a look of grim determination on his face.

Meanwhile, Murphy was too busy to notice the giant's approach. He had other things on his mind as he leant in close to try and kiss the marshal's wife.

The sound of a loud crack rang out as her palm met with the side of her assailant's face with a solid slap. Next, Zoe bunched her fist to punch him in the face, but Murphy caught her wrist in a cruel grip.

He leered at her. 'I think I'll not be struck again. Mrs. Tilghman.'

He was about to try again when a large hand clamped on his shoulder. Murphy turned his head and looked up, and up, to stare into the stern features of Little Joe.

The big man shook his head. 'Nope.'

Murphy released his grip on Zoe who wrenched herself away from the vile creature who thought to accost her. An enraged expression settled on her face and her response was akin to a threatened bear. 'You leave me alone or I'll kill you myself.'

Murphy laughed almost maniacally as she climbed to her feet and stormed off towards the hill.

When she topped the rise, Zoe was taken aback by the chaos before her. It wasn't a fight. It was a wild melee. Even the prison guards were involved. She ran her furious gaze over the crowd as she looked for her husband.

'For the love of God, Bill, where are you?'

Then she saw him. In the middle of it all with Bat Masterson. Both men wading through the chaos handing out "old school justice".

'You just can't help yourself, can you?' Zoe muttered and started down the hill.

She'd reached the edge of the carnage when a man reeled out of it all on drunken legs, blood running from a small cut above his eye. He stopped a matter of inches from the furious Zoe Tilghman and blinked to clear his vision.

When he realized who it was, he opened his mouth to speak.

Zoe on the other hand, was in no mood for more issues with the opposite sex.

'Not now, Pepper,' she snarled and dropped him with a right cross that a prizefighter would have been proud of.

Then, hoisting up her skirts, Zoe stepped around the fallen man, and stormed into the crowd.

When Woody Jeffries appeared through the crowd, Tilghman saw immediately that he carried a cut-down shotgun. The gunsmith tossed it to him and shouted above the din, 'Special load!'

Tilghman knew all about Woody's special loads and nodded his thanks. He thumbed back the hammers, aimed, and let rip with the first barrel.

The unlucky recipient was Arkansas Tom. The outlaw let out a screech of pain and clutched at his butt cheeks where the rock salt had peppered them.

Tilghman switched his aim and sighted on his second target.

'Sorry kid,' he mumbled and let go the other barrel.

Chuck Tilghman seemed to lift four-feet off the ground when the rock salt slammed into his rump. He howled and danced from the burning pain.

Masterson and Woody stood beside him. Both winced and blew out a lung-full of air.

'That was cruel, Bill,' Woody observed wisely. 'Your own son.'

'He's an officer of the law and should behave as such.'

All around, the fighting had come to a halt. Some of the combatants lay on the ground, bloodied and battered. Others were still on their feet although barely.

Masterson said, 'Well, Bill, what we've got is barely controlled chaos.'

Tilghman's face was grim. 'Filming starts Sunday, Bat, and it can't come soon enough.'

Suddenly, Zoe appeared and thrust herself into her husband's arms. She was visibly upset.

'What's up, Zoe? Are you OK?' he asked in a concerned voice.

'Just Murphy acting the fool. Can we just go home?'

'What's that son of a bitch done, Zoe?' Tilghman grated.

'It's nothing. I want to go home.'

'Sure.'

As the crowd started to disperse they walked back over the hill and towards their buckboard. Momma and Frankie were already there waiting, along with Tench and Malachi.

Chuck appeared with Becky. She was dabbing blood away from his face while he clutched at his buttocks. Every time he did, he gave a sorrowful moan.

'Shut up, you deserve it,' Becky snapped. 'Such an embarrassing display of manners out in public.'

Chuck looked at his father. He gave him a bewildered look. 'You shot me.'

Tilghman nodded. 'As the girl said, you deserved it.'

Zoe punched Bill on the arm. 'You shot your son?'

'It was only rock salt. One of Woody's special loads,' he explained. 'He's an officer of the law. Maybe next time he'll behave like one. Get on the wagon, Chuck.'

Chuck felt his tender posterior once more and grimaced. 'I'll walk if it's all the same.'

Tench stepped forward and gave Chuck back his gun.

Tilghman stared at his son. 'We'll talk about that later, too.' He turned to Zoe. 'You'll have to drive home. I need to stay and see that all the prisoners get back to the hotel. I'll ride Chuck's horse home.'

Zoe wasn't happy and her expression told him so. 'OK. But, don't be too long.'

A couple of wagons back, the outlaws were being loaded up under the watchful gaze of some wounded guards.

Melton looked at Younger who was standing to one side, and motioned to him. 'Time to go, Mr. Younger.'

'Coming, sir.'

As he was about to climb aboard, Murphy stepped in close and whispered, 'Cole Younger, you sir, are up to something.'

Younger ignored him.

Murphy placed a hand on his arm. 'Let me in on it.'

The outlaw looked at the hand and then at Murphy. 'In due time, my good man. All in due time. Now remove your hand before I break your fingers.'

Arkansas Tom leaned in close. 'I hope whatever you are scheming is going to take Tilghman down a peg.'

Younger climbed onto the wagon and looked down at them. *'There are more things in heaven and earth than are dreamt of in your philosophy.'*

Arkansas Tom looked at Murphy. 'What?'

'Don't worry, you wouldn't understand.'

Tilghman now sat atop Chuck's horse and eyed the outlaws with suspicion. No matter how hard he tried, he couldn't shake the feeling that they were up to something.

Catching Murphy Jones looking at him, the outlaw gave him a gleeful smile. Before this was over, he realized, he was going to have to kill him.

When Cole Younger entered his room, he knew what to expect, thanks to the clerk on the desk down stairs.

He opened the door, and from across the room, saw her looking out the window at the street below.

He closed the door behind himself and said, '*Age cannot wither her, nor custom stale her infinite variety.*'

Alice turned back to the bed and started to put more clothing into her suitcase. 'You know, in all of our time together, I've never believed a word you've said. But I sure love hearing you say them.'

'Seems that neither of us could shed the other.'

'Seems so. I quit trying to make sense of it. I just show up to do your bidding and leave not knowing when I'll ever lay eyes on you again. Months. Years. Never.'

'No need to leave just yet.'

She stared at him. 'I think it best.'

He moved in closer to Alice, grasped her arms and pulled her close. 'What if we…?'

Alice pulled away from him. 'Not this time, Cole. Don't feel right. Another year and you would be a free man. Yet something tells me you're going to throw it all away. Couldn't stand by and watch it.'

Anger flashed in Younger's eyes. 'Free man? Free to do what? Die in the dark, alone and forgotten.'

The hurt in Alice's eyes was unmistakable. She slammed the case shut and snapped, 'Goodbye, Cole.'

Before she walked out of the room, Alice reached down beside her case and picked up a book. 'I did what you asked me to.'

She handed it to him. On the cover it read, **The Complete Works of Shakespeare**.

Alice kissed Younger on the cheek, picked up her case, and without looking back, walked silently from the room. As the door closed, he opened his mouth to call her back, but nothing came out.

Younger felt a pang of loss for a time as he stood there all alone. He stared again at the book in his hands and opened it. In the hollowed-out section within was a box of Colt cartridges.

He opened the box and took out a single round. He held it before his eyes then shifted his gaze towards the closed door. For an instant Younger entertained the idea of going after Alice, but then his eyes were drawn back to the bullet.

His mind started to wander.

Another place, another time.

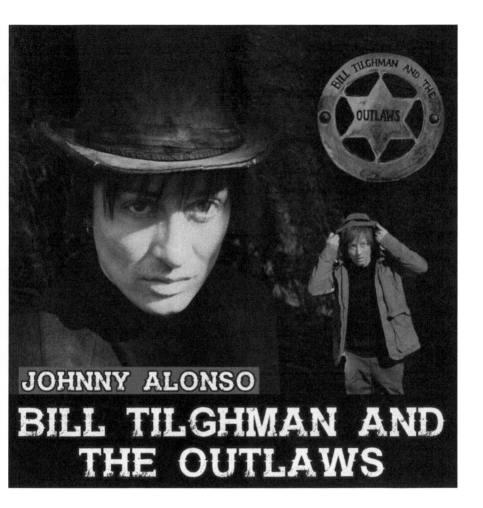

KEN ARNOLD

BILL TILGHMAN AND
THE OUTLAWS

BRIAN ST. AUGUST

BILL TILGHMAN AND THE OUTLAWS

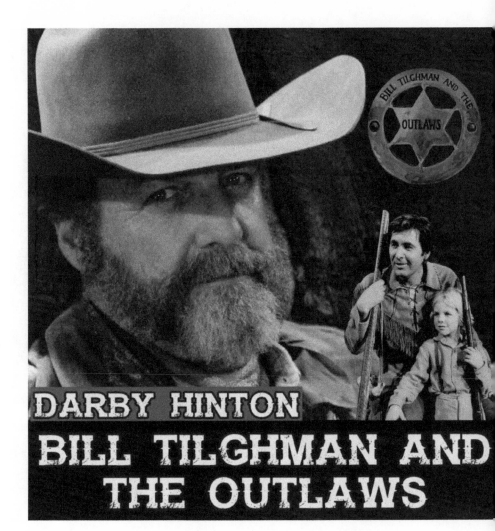

DARBY HINTON

BILL TILGHMAN AND THE OUTLAWS

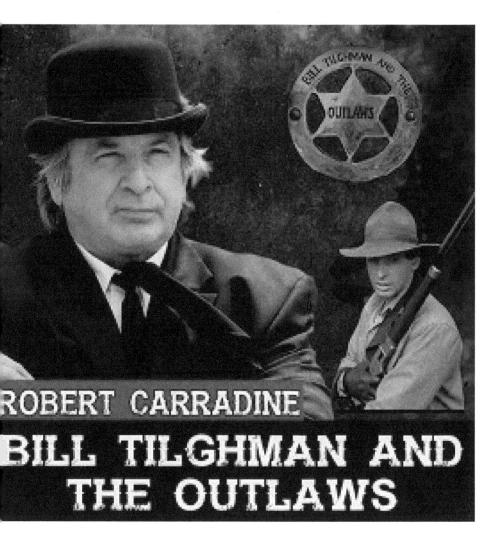

ROBERT CARRADINE

BILL TILGHMAN AND THE OUTLAWS

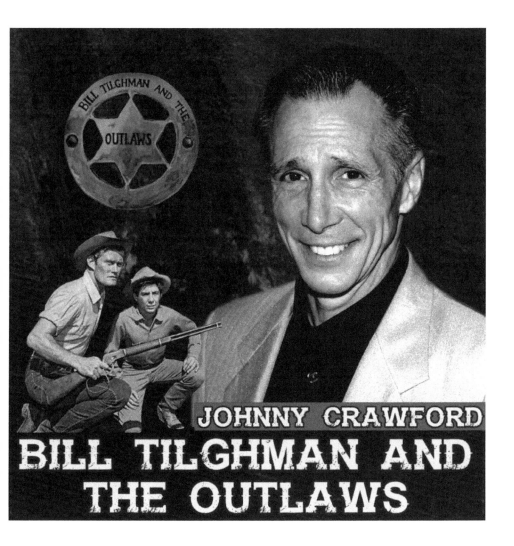

JOHNNY CRAWFORD

BILL TILGHMAN AND THE OUTLAWS

EIGHT

The following morning the main street of Fort Bowers was a hive of activity. Camera and lighting crews went about their business with a stoic determination, getting set up for the coming day.

Keeping an eye on the gathered crowd were Tilghman, Bear, Masterson, and a sorry looking Chuck.

Two stuntmen were practicing a fight sequence in a large patch of bright, morning sunlight, which everyone seemed to be oblivious of. Except for one man.

'Get a load of these two Nancys, will you,' William growled. 'I swear they've had more swings than Larry Doyle and not one of them has landed.'

'What else do you expect, he plays for the darned New York Giants,' Red growled.

Boyd frowned. 'What in tarnation are they doing?'

William dragged himself to his feet from where he'd been sitting with his friends on their favorite bench seat. He shook his head and shouted at the larger of the two men, 'Hit him, you big sissy. Old Red here could beat both you fellas and not even get off his stool.'

William broke out into a wracking cough and his face turned scarlet. He staggered back and sat down.

His friends looked concerned and Red asked, 'Are you all right?'

William coughed some more, hawked, and spat on the boardwalk between his feet. In the middle of the wet patch wriggled a small, black insect. 'Darn fly tried to kill me.'

Boyd shook his head. 'I always knew that mouth of yours was too big.'

Red noted Selig and Gulman as they ambled past on their way to the saloon. The former seemed to be studying some kind of board in his hands.

As they were moving past them, Red said, 'Fine morning. Mr. Selig.'

Selig paused from looking at the notes on his ever-present clipboard and smiled at him. 'My friend, it's a fine day to make a movie. I tell you what, if you gentlemen remain seated here, you may just find yourselves on the silver screen. So, don't move.'

Red smiled at the thought of seeing himself on one of the flicker pictures. 'We'll stay right here.'

Boyd agreed. 'That would be mighty fine.'

William, however, looked at him and asked, 'How long you going to be? I need a trip to the privy!'

Selig chuckled and winked at Red. 'Heaven forbid we should hold up nature, my man. I'll put things on hold until you get back.'

William nodded and struggled to his feet. 'I'll be right back, fellas. Don't start the filming without me.'

All of them laughed. Selig said, 'I'll leave you to your ablutions, sir.'

After the two men were gone Boyd stared at William. 'A refined gentleman you ain't.'

The latter mumbled a few incoherent words and kept walking. The privy called.

Meanwhile, Selig and Gulman entered the Tilghman-Masterson Saloon. Inside they discovered Frank James measuring up Younger for a new shirt. The man was bare-chested and Hathaway seemed to be paying more attention than usual to what was going on.

So, too, was Melody. She seemed quite content watching Russell as he sat back, picking a tune on his guitar, than taking any interest to the notes on her clipboard.

All the Joes, plus Murphy Jones, and Old Joe's wife, Miss Darling, sat at a rear table while a poor-looking Arkansas Tom, along with Cherokee Waite and Billy Sunset, sat at a table not far away.

The guards, too, had not escaped the previous day's festivities lightly either, which was noticeable as they stood watch over the exits.

Selig looked around the room, took a deep breath and said, loud enough for all to hear, 'Gentlemen, and Ladies, I can't tell you how excited I am to get this project under way. Since for all of you this is your first experience with moving pictures, I want to explain to you how this all works.'

Gulman jumped in, excitement on his face. 'Yes, yes, yes. It's art like no other. We start with nothing and ...'

Selig cut him off. '... And in two weeks we have a picture show that will excite thousands. Right now, you will all be fitted for costumes and, outside, our crew is already hard at work determining where to set up the cameras.'

There was movement at the top of the stairs and Fletcher the armorer appeared. He was a solidly-built man in his forties and his broad shoulders carried the gun belts he had draped over them quite well. In his left hand he carried a Winchester rifle.

As he clomped down the stairs, Selig indicated to him. 'You have already met Mr. Fletcher, who is in charge of our arsenal.'

Gulman showed a wry smile as he said, 'I wanted to use real bullets, but—'

Fletcher dumped his load of blanks on a table and took out a cartridge. He held it up for them all to see. 'But, Mr. Gulman will have to settle for blanks. It's my job to avert any accidents. No one on or off the set, except our guards, will have live ammunition. Just before any scenes in which guns are fired, I will hand each of you an empty .45 Colt and six black powder blanks.'

'Thank you, Mr. Fletcher. Mr. Gulman will give you a brief summary of the action.'

Gulman started to speak, 'Pay close attention. It is a beautiful spring morning. The birds are singing, children play in the streets and the folks are going about their business. When suddenly—'

Selig interrupted, 'Mr. Gulman, remember you are talking to the actors not the audience.'

'Of course. Our desperadoes, the scourge of the west whose black hearts seethe with malicious intent—'

'Thank you, Mr. Gulman,' Selig said, chopping the man's words off again. He stepped over to an aerial ground plot that had been placed up on a table for all to see. 'For our big scene we will have our antagonists, that's you, staged in three different areas. Miss Hathaway will go over all of that with you tomorrow. One thing that is so difficult about film making is that we often shoot out of sequence. We will start with the most difficult scenes first, the robbery itself. We'll take two days to rehearse the robbery, then cameras will roll the next day.'

Gulman gave them all a stern stare. 'It is very important that you stand where you are told to. This is your mark. You move and you will ruin the composition of my shot!'

Selig said. 'Film, my friends, is forever. And regardless of what fate has in store for us, "Bill Tilghman and the Outlaws" will be our legacy. Now it's time to prepare. Miss Hathaway and Melody.'

Selig turned and started to walk outside, Gulman and the ladies following.

Fletcher, on the other hand, was about to go back upstairs when he was stopped by Cole Younger. 'Mr. Fletcher, may I see one of your blank cartridges?'

The armorer reached into his pocket and took out a blank cartridge. He stared at it briefly and then tossed it to the outlaw. Younger caught it in his right hand.

He examined it and was about to toss it back to Fletcher who held up a hand. 'Keep it.'

Younger nodded his thanks and watched the armorer turn and climb the stairs.

Murphy moved out of his seat once Fletcher was gone and walked across to Younger and Frank James, under the watchful eyes of the guards.

He stared at the scars on Younger's chest. 'Damn! I never do get used to seeing that mess of scars.'

'Twenty-one ghosts that continue to haunt. Eleven from Northfield alone. Not our best idea, huh Frank?'

'Yet, here you stand. Body and soul.'

'Evidently.'

There was a pregnant pause before Murphy turned away and took a cigarette from his pocket.

Behind him, Younger started to put his shirt on. He said to Frank, 'Well, Frank, at least I am going to look good while Tilghman humiliates me for all the world to see. The up side is they might be able to make me look twenty years younger.'

'Too late for us all I think,' Frank said.

'Maybe. But perhaps not too late to set it right.'

Frank frowned. 'Set what right, Cole?'

'Northfield, Minnesota.'

'Northfield?' Frank shook his head. 'There's no setting that right. They knew we were coming. We didn't have a chance from the minute we stepped out of the bank. Cost us dearly. We both carry the scars.'

Younger's voice grew quiet, menacing. 'I need to set it right, Frank, and this might be our chance. And the bonus is knocking that self-righteous Bill Tilghman off his high horse.'

'Sounds illegal, Cole.'

'There is nothing either good or bad, but thinking makes it so.'

'Enough of the Shakespeare, Cole. Every action has a consequence.'

'Maybe so, but we were alive then, Frank. Hell, they were writing books about us. "The Robin Hoods of the West." Now, we are just fodder for the likes of Bill Tilghman. Forgotten relics of a forgotten time.'

'Damn it, Cole, life is good now. I have my own shop… make a living wage.'

Frank saw Younger's skeptical look and continued, 'And I am bored, out of my mind. Everyday measuring and stitching like some old maid. I am respected, … but stand for nothing. God, help me, what do you have in mind, dear Satan?'

'What if we rob the bank … for real?'

'Why?'

Murphy had gone nowhere and after overhearing their conversation, turned back around. 'To humiliate the great Bill

Tilghman. If he has his way, we become laughing stocks. Arrested and jailed for all to see. Hell, even my Momma will think I'm a fool.'

'On the other hand, if we turn the tables and rob the bank for real … then it's Tilghman and Masterson who become the fools and we become the legends,' Younger said, confirming what Murphy had said.

'We could get ourselves killed,' Frank said stoically.

Murphy glared at Frank. 'I have no intention of dying unless Tilghman goes with me.'

Suddenly, the quiet background piano music played by Curly grew in intensity. Younger whirled towards him and snarled, 'What, pray tell is that racket? I swear if I had a gun…'

Curly mumbled something under his breath and returned to playing it quietly. Younger turned to Frank. 'Are you in?'

Frank hesitated momentarily, but then nodded. 'I long to be alive, Cole, even more than I long to live. Of course, I'm in. How do you see this one playing itself out?'

Ignoring Murphy, Younger leaned in close to Frank and whispered into his ear. Frank's expression changed gradually until a broad grin split his aged face.

By now, Murphy was feeling put out. He growled, 'I don't know how you are planning to pull this off, gentlemen, but I want in.'

Five minutes later, Younger, Frank, and Murphy sat at a table with Old Joe and Miss Darling.

'So, we are the only ones with real bullets and a pretty, little bank right in front of us, just waiting to be robbed?' Frank questioned.

Younger nodded.

Old Joe shook his head. 'Count me out, Cole. I'm going straight. I just don't have the heart for robbing no more.'

Miss Darling, however, had other ideas. 'Joe, I told you all that Bible reading was going to mess up your thinking. This is our chance.'

Younger looked across at the table where Arkansas Tom and the others were seated. Standing beside them was Pepper, who'd brought in a tray of pastries for them to eat.

'Pepper, bring that tray over here,' Younger called to him.

When he reached the table, Younger asked in a low voice, 'Pepper, can we trust you?'

Pepper looked hesitantly around the room. 'Oh, yes, sir. Yes, sir. Just ask and it's done.'

'We're going to need a diversion.'

Pepper frowned.

Younger sighed. 'Something big and loud.'

Pepper smiled. 'I can do that.'

A time later, everyone had gathered outside on the street. There was a buzz of excitement from the crowd as anticipation built about the start of rehearsals. Tilghman stood watching as Miss Hathaway appeared on the boardwalk and demanded everybody's attention.

'Ladies and Gentlemen,' she called, then waited patiently for all eyes to focus on her. 'If you were thinking I was here as just another pretty face, before we're finished you'll know better. What we are going to do here is, quite frankly, impossible.'

A murmur of confusion rippled through the crowd.

Hathaway continued, 'We have scheduled ten days, in which we will plan and execute a daring bank robbery, a dangerous chase, a deadly shoot out; all culminating in a dramatic trial of some of the most nefarious desperadoes to ever stalk the west. Before we are finished, you will be poked and prodded, you will wallow in the dirt; you will collapse at night, exhausted, only to get up the next day to do it all over again.

For the next two days we will rehearse the bank robbery. Then on Sunday, we will shoot the scene. On Monday, we rehearse and shoot the Outlaws entering town. Tuesday, Mr. Tilghman and his posse pursue the robbers. We will then take a three-day siesta to recover from our fourteen hour work days and then ... On Day six we will rehearse the deadly shoot out and then film it on Day seven.

On Day eight, the trial. And I know it makes no sense, but Day nine will be spent working on the filming of the desperadoes in their hideout where they plan the robbery. Day ten is open for anything we still need to shoot. Any questions?'

'Could you repeat that, Miss Hathaway?'

Hathaway's eyes burned into Masterson which caused him to raise a hand in surrender.

'On second thoughts, I think I have it.'

Laughter came from the crowd as Masterson shrank back.

'We can also expect Wyatt Earp and Bass Reeves to join us before we are finished.'

Hathaway's announcement brought forth a ripple of excitement from the onlookers. Then her voice hardened. 'Every morning we meet here at exactly 6 a.m. to get instructions for the day. Now, step to it.'

The rest of the first day was a blur of set up, orders, and trying to get shots right. To Tilghman it was all unnecessary chaos and it concerned him. For the outlaws, the seemingly organized disorganization gave them the chance to start piecing together their

plan.

NINE

That night in the Blenderhassett Hotel, all the outlaws were spent and in their rooms when Frank arrived with two costumes on hangers. He was on his way to the stairs when the guard, Ross stopped him.

'What's going on, Mr. James? I thought you'd be wore out like the rest of them.'

'I've got a couple of costumes to fit for Murphy Jones and Cole Younger.'

Ross nodded. 'I'll have to escort you up.'

'Lead the way, my good man.'

At the top of the stairs they proceeded along the hall until they were at Murphy's room. Ross put his head inside, said some words, and Murphy appeared. Once they were at Younger's room, Ross let them in and stood guard outside the door.

From inside, Ross heard Frank say in a raised voice, 'Need you both to try these on before I hem them up.'

Ross smiled as Younger moaned, 'I'm tuckered, Frank. Tomorrow. Can't we...'

'Oh, quit your belly aching and put these on. You too, Murphy.'

Inside, Frank motioned to them to move towards the back of the room. He said in a low voice, 'I'm not sure we can pull this off. Must be a hundred people. Only takes one to upset the cart. You know, I got a lot more to lose than both of you.'

'No time to get cold feet, Frank,' Murphy sneered.

Younger picked up his book and opened it to reveal the live .45 rounds. 'Look, Frank, it's a cake walk. By the end of tomorrow, we'll know every move. What's more, you and I will have the only guns that bark.'

'What about me?' Murphy snapped.

Younger stared at him. 'Don't want a slaughter house, Murphy. I want you and your men to disarm the guards. They'll be out of sight. Easy pickings. You and your men will have their rifles.' Younger's voice grew cold. 'Listen, Murphy, you shed a drop of blood and I'll kill you myself.'

Murphy held his stare for a few heartbeats before saying, 'I'll play it your way, Cole, but I want Tilghman. He's mine.'

Ignoring Murphy's comment, Younger switched his gaze to Frank. 'I'll fill in Old Joe and his brood tomorrow. But I'm leaving the kid out of this. He'll cave I'm sure. Besides, he's so moon-eyed over Selig's daughter, I can't trust him. Gulman has the kid holding our horses near the livery. What more could we want? We'll beat it out of town and leave him scratching his head.'

'How do I get my share?' Murphy asked.

Younger gave the killer a hard look. 'Check the barrel outside the livery. It will be there. Something else to chew on, Murphy, take the money and hightail it. Save Tilghman for another day. Let him play the fool awhile.'

'I'll play that hand as it's dealt.'

For a moment, anger flared in Younger's eyes. He wished he had a damned Colt to put the live rounds in. Then he could place a slug in Murphy's head, the cold son of a bitch.

Sensing the tension, Frank moved towards the door. 'Thank you, gentlemen. You will be decked out for the cover of the Saturday Evening Post when I'm done with you.'

Ross opened the door. 'You finished?'

Frank nodded. 'Indeed I am.'

The dawn of day two found Tilghman sauntering along the boardwalk as he did early morning rounds. He'd had a restless night, so decided to perform the job a deputy normally would. All along the boardwalk the shopkeepers were putting out items for sale, ready for the coming day.

'Waste of time,' Tilghman muttered, 'if it's anything like yesterday.'

A wagon rattled along the street, leaving early before the thoroughfare became choked with people. Up ahead he saw Woody Jeffries emerge from his gun shop.

Woody caught sight of Tilghman and gave him a wave. 'Morning, Marshal.'

'Morning.'

'It's quiet now, but all hell will break loose shortly,' Woody observed. 'Do you see something different, Marshal?'

'Lucky if I can see anything these days.'

'Someone pilfered my cannon.'

'Any idea who?'

Woody shook his head. 'Could've been kids.'

Tilghman shook his head. 'I got my doubts. To tell you the truth, I wish we had never started all of this.'

Woody concurred, 'I wish Bass and Wyatt were here. When are they due in?'

'In a couple of days, when we chase the outlaws.'

'I imagine they are in Sweetwater by now.'

'No doubt,' Tilghman agreed. 'More than likely holed up at the Red Bull Saloon.'

'Hmm, I got a call to make.'

Woody walked back inside the store and out into the back room where the Western Union telephone hung on the wall. He picked up the earpiece and turned it, cranked the handle, and waited for the operator.

After a moment the familiar voice of Mabel came down the line to him. 'Hey, handsome. What's on your mind so early this morning?'

Woody smiled at the tone in her voice. The pair were well acquainted with each other. 'Not what you're thinking, Mabel.'

'Too bad. Your loss.'

'I'll make it up to you. Mabel, But right now, I need to get in touch with Wyatt Earp. He is at the Red Bull Saloon in Sweetwater.'

'Wyatt Earp?' Mabel went quiet for a moment before she asked, 'Can't it wait until Ethel's shift starts? I'd rather not make that call.'

'Mabel, just ring Sweetwater. Would you, please?'

Mabel sighed. 'Okay, Johnny, hold tight.'

The bartender in the Red Bull was named Sam Higgins and, at the time the phone on the wall rang, he was shifting a keg of beer in preparation for the coming day.

There were only two other people in the barroom at that time. One was asleep on the sofa against one of the timber-paneled walls. The other sat at a polished-topped table with his head resting on his arms. Marshals Wyatt Earp and Bass Reeves.

Sam shook his head. 'Man, you old fellers sure tied one on last night.'

'I heard that,' Bass mumbled.

The phone rang.

And rang.

And rang.

'You got but a moment to stop that noisy contraption before I kill it,' Wyatt growled without opening his eyes.

Sam picked up. 'Yeah?'

'Sam, I need to speak with Wyatt Earp. Is he in Sweetwater?'

Sam rolled his eyes. 'I'll see if I can arrange that without him or Bass shooting me.'

'I need to speak with them both.'

'Wyatt, it's for you.'

Wyatt cracked an eye. 'I knew I shoulda shot it right off.'

He clambered slowly to his feet, his thin frame protesting all the way. Now in his sixties, his hair was white and thinning by the day. His face was deeply lined, and his mustache now matched the winter snows.

He took the earpiece. 'Yeah?'

'Wyatt, this is Mabel, the operator over in Fort Bowers.'

Wyatt smiled. 'Mabel, Mabel, Mabel. Mabel, you know I got married, right?'

'Wyatt! For heaven's sake, Woody Jeffries wants to speak with you.'

Wyatt massaged his temple. 'Oh, sorry.'

'Is Bass there with you, Wyatt?'

'Sure is. I'll fetch him.'

Wyatt waved at Bass who now sat back in his chair, a dazed look on his face.

'What do you want?' he growled in his baritone voice.

Wyatt pointed at the phone. 'Bass, come over here and stick your ear to this phone with me. Woody and Mabel are on the party line.'

'I knew I should never've agreed to this,' he rumbled, climbing to his feet.

Even in his later years, with bald pate, grey mustache, and lined features, the famous deputy marshal still cut an imposing figure. Then he walked.

He lurched forward, teetered, and then gathered himself. 'Lord, help me. Last time I go anywhere with you.'

Bass took the earpiece. 'This is Bass Reeves.'

'This is Bass Reeves,' he repeated.

'Mr. Reeves, I have Woody Jeffries on the line for you.'

Bass' eyes lit up. 'Mabel, Mabel, Mabel, you sweet flower, it's been too long.'

'Not now, Bass. Woody's on the line. Pay attention, for heaven's sake.'

Surprised, Bass gathered himself and said, 'Uh hey, Woody, what's going on?'

Woody's voice came through the earpiece. 'Like to talk to you both for just a minute.'

'Sure, go.'

'What are the chances of you two getting here a day early? Things are getting interesting. I have the feeling Tilghman would rest easier if you were both here. These picture-folk have turned Fort Bowers upside down.'

Wyatt said, 'Well, we could try. It'll mean riding a lot harder than we're used to these days.'

Bass rolled his eyes.

'You know we've got Cole Younger and eight other troublemakers here, including that no-good, Murphy Jones?'

Wyatt frowned. 'Murphy's a hard case bowl of nuts. Have they lost their minds?'

'Seems the whole town has movie fever, Wyatt. There might be trouble. I just thought I'd ask.'

'We'll try, Woody.'

'I'll see you then.'

They both hung up and Wyatt turned to his friend. 'What do you say, Bass?'

'Let's ride.'

TEN

As the morning progressed, Tilghman wasn't the only one with concerns. As Selig and Melody weaved their way through the hive of activity, the producer caught his daughter looking at Russell. The young woman seemed to be falling in love and the man who'd taken her eye was a convicted criminal.

He stopped. 'Melody, darling, I've been watching you with Russell. That convict they call Chicken Man.'

'Daddy, the charges that got John put in prison are just a lot of nonsense.'

Selig nodded. 'Even the Warden mentioned that the kid didn't belong there. But regardless, what do you see in this fellow?'

Melody's eyes turned misty. 'Daddy, he is sweet, kind. He would like more than anything to get his mother and little brother and start a new life somewhere. Raise a family…'

Alarm shot through Selig. 'Girl, what are you hoping this will lead to?'

She shrugged. 'I don't really know. But I like that he makes me laugh.'

'You know, sweetheart, I've already lost your mother and I simply couldn't bear losing you too.'

Melody's eyes softened at the mention of her mother. 'Oh, Daddy.'

'I know I'm an idiot, but I'm an idiot who loves you.'

She patted him on the hand and nodded towards the bank. 'Come on. We've got a movie to make.'

When they reached the bank, Tilghman, Masterson, and the deputies were there waiting. So, too, were the outlaws.

Woody Jeffries had been hired by Fletcher to help with the firearms. His thoughts were, when good help is on hand, why not use it?

Together they'd passed out weapons to those who required them. But, when Fletcher walked past Gulman, the director put out his hand and motioned to the one six-gun that the armorer carried.

Hesitantly, Fletcher gave it to him.

Gulman raised it into the air and tried to fire it to get everyone's attention. Nothing happened. He tried again, and again, and again, and again. By the fifth try, all present were staring at his clumsy attempts to fire the weapon.

Hathaway stepped forward and gently relieved him of it before he hurt himself, raised it in the air and expertly fired off a round. She then handed it back to Fletcher, catching his eye and giving her head a slight shake. She whispered, 'Please don't let him have another one.'

Now that he had their attention, however, Gulman moved on. '*Action!* Moving pictures demand *Action!* You remember, Mr. James and Mr. Younger will enter the bank. You and you and you,' he said as he pointed at Old Joe, Big Joe and Little Joe, 'will be on horseback outside the bank, looking out for the law.'

The three nodded.

Gulman continued. He waved his hands at Murphy, Arkansas Tom, Billy Sunset and Cherokee Waite. 'You four will be spread out around the town, rifles ready. And you,' he said to Russell, 'will be at the livery holding *eins, zwei, drei* horses.'

He held up three fingers.

'After Mr. Goldstein, … He is the banker in our film, is shot, Mr. James and Mr. Younger exit the bank, guns blazing. Mr. Tilghman and his deputies will run out of the jail and Mr. Tilghman will point his gun at the first outlaw he sees.' Gulman's eyes settled on Murphy, '*You!* You, Mr. Jones will shoot and miss Mr. Tilghman and he will then shoot you.'

Murphy's jaw hardened. 'What if I don't cotton to getting shot by the marshal?'

Selig missed the warning sign and said placatingly, 'Don't worry, Mr. Jones, it's just a movie.'

Murphy ignored him. All he could think about was his chance to kill Tilghman.

Later that afternoon, just as the last of the sun's orange fingers were about to disappear below the distant horizon, two old lawmen slid from their saddles and staggered around as though they'd been beaten steadily with sticks. Riding horses hard for hours seemed a task best left to the young.

Both Wyatt and Bass cursed the name Bill Tilghman as they set up camp for the night.

An hour later, Bass was leaning against his saddle and Wyatt was stirring the fire under the coffee pot when the former said, 'We still have twenty-five miles to go. Not sure these old bones would survive if I had to get back on that old jughead tonight.'

Wyatt nodded. 'Ain't that the truth. If we leave first thing in the morning, we will still be there a day early, just as Woody asked. You know, I'm thinking this flicker business has its appeal. You get paid for pretending to be shot at and no one ever dies. You know, I've been getting calls from movie folk. Why just last month some guy named Griffith wanted me to advise for a moving picture. Don't know what to make of it.'

'They ain't calling on me, I guarantee you that. Ain't seen a black man in a movie yet that weren't a clown or a fool. Lots of Injuns, but even they look white. Not even sure why Tilghman wants me. Bet that Hollywood fella don't even know I'm black.'

Wyatt looked incredulous. 'Hell, cowboys come in all colors, except green. In fact, that old, rancher Tom Goodman has fifteen cowhands, all black or Mexican, except for the foreman. And he's a red-headed Irishman. Bass, you just might be the first black man on the big screen.'

Bass snorted. 'Shining boots, maybe.'

Wyatt's face grew serious. 'No, as Bass Reeves. The man who nailed the Brunter brothers.'

'That'll be the day. You know, one of those sorry sons of bitches, I think it was Harvey Brunter, shot off my gun belt.'

Wyatt frowned. 'He what?'

'Yep, true as I'm sitting. Butch Brunter tore up my arrest warrant and started slinging lead.'

'All of them Brunters were crazy and mean.'

Bass nodded. 'Yep. Had to drop them all, but Butch. By now my gun belt was around my knees with Butch yanking on his gun, not ten feet away. The thing was hung up in his belt, thank God. So here I am, gun empty, as knocked-kneed as a preacher's kid, trying to get to Butch before he cleared his holster. Good thing Butch was slow. I stumbled over and clubbed the fool. Down he went. You know, Butch wasn't all that bad.'

'Now that should be in pictures.'

'Not unless I wake up a red-haired Irishman. … Ain't right." Bass looked into a dark box he chose not to visit very often. "Well, we ain't solving all the world's injustices here tonight, are we old friend?'

Wyatt, trying to change the mood, said, 'You may not wake up Irish, but men our age are lucky to wake up at all.'

Both men laughed.

'Ain't that the truth. If you wake before me in the morning, check

to see if I'm still breathing. I wake up first, I'll do the same for you.'

They laughed again and then sat there in silence.

ELEVEN

The third morning was just as chaotic as the day before. Except this time, it was slightly more of an organized chicken chase.

Selig stood off to one side and watched as the magic of movie making unfolded. The outlaws were split into three groups.

Murphy Jones, Arkansas Tom, Billy Sunset, and Cherokee Waite were in the first. Younger and James, dressed in business attire, were the second, while Old Joe, Little Joe and Big Joe, who all wore dusters, were the third.

Fletcher and Johnny handed out ammunition to them while they waited for further instructions.

Red, Boyd, and William sat on the bench seat outside the bank which meant, come action time, the three old timers were in a prime position to watch the action unfold.

The Tilghman family plus Malachi were all dressed as background extras and were outside the general store loading a wagon. Minus, Bill, however.

Tilghman, Masterson, and their deputies were outside the jail, while most of the townsfolk acted as extras. Those that weren't, just watched from afar.

Then the guards moved the outlaws into position and they were about set to go.

Melody was standing quietly with her father when she spotted one of the stage hands give Russell three horses to hold. She glanced briefly to see her father watching everything going on, and walked over to stand with the prisoner.

He smiled warmly at her and she placed her hand on his shoulder. 'Aren't you excited?'

Russell shrugged. 'All I got to do is hold the horses. Nothing exciting about that.'

'Just wait until the dramatic chase, galloping horses, roaring guns.'

'When's that?'

'In a couple of days.'

Russell gave Melody a solemn look. 'I wish it were a couple of weeks.'

She frowned. 'A couple of weeks?'

Russell hesitated, then said, 'I'd spend as much time with you as I can.'

'Why, John Russell, you're not suggesting …?'

'I ain't suggesting, I'm saying …' his voice trailed away.

'What are you saying?'

Just then they were interrupted by one of the stage hands. 'Mr. Russell, you need to get into position.'

Russell stared at Melody before he turned and started to walk away. Melody called after him, 'I'm very interested in hearing what you have to say.'

'I don't believe it! Why in the hell does everything happen to me?' Pepper swore at his bad luck. He had no cannonball to ram into Woody Jeffries' cannon.

It had taken him forever to get it up on the ridge that overlooked the town. He'd loaded it with powder; too much he'd find out later, and now he didn't have the shot to go in it.

'What are you going to do now, Pepper? You danged goose.'

He stood in silence and scratched his head. Then he saw it. Finally, fate, or so it seemed, had smiled down on old Pepper. A rock. He frowned and stared at the cannon again.

Could it?

Pepper shrugged and picked the rock up and placed it at the mouth of the barrel. He then went and found more, ramming them as he went, until he was satisfied he had enough.

Now he needed to wait for the right time.

'Action!' Gulman's voice blared through the megaphone from his position atop a scaffold.

Cameras started to roll, people moved about the set as rehearsed, and Murphy and his men made their move.

Each took out one guard a piece and kept their weapons for themselves. They also relieved them of the ammunition and dropped the spares into their pockets.

Near the livery, Russell held the reins of three horses, oblivious of what was happening.

The Joes stood next to the bank and waited patiently for what they knew was to come. They watched on as Younger and Frank approached the bank and climbed the steps. They paused outside and looked around, looking to see if everyone was in position. When Younger saw they were, he and Frank walked inside …

… And stopped dead.

Before them stood a bald man of average height and build, a broad smile on his face which advertised his excitement.

'Who are you?' Younger snapped.

'I'm Mort,' Mort said excitedly. 'This is so exciting.'

Younger saw the bags of fake money beside him on the counter.

'Anyone else here?'

'No, just us.'

Just then, Hathaway stuck her head through the door. 'Give us a few minutes, gentlemen, while we reset cameras. When we call 'Action' that's your cue, Mr. Goldstein. Mr. Younger and Mr. James, your cue will be Mr. Gulman calling 'Now.' You then exit the bank. And remember, guns blazing.'

She withdrew her head and closed the door, then Younger turned his attention back to Mort, a scowl on his face.

Mort said, 'My part is coming up.'

He turned away and started to rehearse his lines. Behind him, Frank and Younger looked at each other and shrugged. Then they began to change out their loads for the real thing.

While they did so, Mort turned around. He frowned when he saw what they were doing and stopped. Younger and James both put a finger to their mouths and whispered, 'Shhhh ...' He looked around at the faces of the men gathered and frowned some more, then his eyes widened.

The bank robbery was no longer play acting; these men were actually going to rob the bank!

From outside he heard Hathaway call out to the rest of the cast and crew. 'Once our robbers exit the bank, there will be gunshots. All of the outlaws will then start shooting as well and all the townsfolk will run for cover.'

Yeah, Mort thought, *they'll really need to run.*

Things outside continued to roll on, the onlookers oblivious to what those inside the bank were up to. Selig approached Tilghman and the others waiting outside the jail and gave them direction. 'Gentlemen, we need you to move inside and remain there until you hear multiple gunshots. At that point you will run out of the jail and into the street towards the bank. Just run past the camera I showed you earlier.'

Tilghman nodded, his unease still evident. Over Selig's shoulder he noticed Murphy and the others approach the bank. He saw the Murphy say something to Hathaway and then disappear inside.

'Marshal?' Selig said.

Without taking his eyes from the bank, Tilghman said, 'Yeah?'

'You need to go inside.'

His eyes snapped back to Selig and he nodded. 'Yeah, right.'

When Murphy walked inside the bank, Younger and Frank turned in time to see him take the gun from inside his coat.

Younger frowned. 'Forgot your place, Murphy?'

The others fanned out behind their boss. A smug look crossed his face and he said, 'No, Cole, I'm exactly where I meant to be all along.'

'That's not the plan, Murphy,' Frank reminded him.

Murphy's eyes moved left. 'There has been a slight change of plans, Frank.'

Younger cocked the six-gun in his hand and Murphy responded in kind.

'We don't need to go there, Cole,' Murphy stated.

'You're the one taking it there.'

Murphy noticed Mort and asked, 'What is your name?'

Mort eyed him warily. But when he spoke, it was with confidence. 'Mordecai Goldstein, sir. Bank detective. Why, I've stopped more robberies than Mr. Younger and Mr. James here have committed in all their born days.'

Younger rolled his eyes.

Murphy gave Mort a skeptical look and asked, 'Is there such a thing as a bank detective? You look more like a teller to me.'

'Part of my disguise.'

Murphy raised his gun. 'Bank detective?'

Mort shook his head violently. 'Nope, teller!'

'Good career path.'

'Yes, sir.'

'Mort, I want you to do me a favor.'

'Yes, sir.'

Murphy took one of the money sacks and emptied the fake money onto the floor. He said, 'My bullets are real, just in case you have any doubts. Now, Mr. Goldstein, go to the safe and fill that bag with

real money.'

'I, I, … I don't know the combination.'

The hammer went back on the six-gun in Murphy's hand.

'Yes, I do!'

Murphy dragged Mort towards him by the collar and whipped the

gun across his cheek, opening a gash from which blood started to

flow freely. 'Don't muck me around, Goldstein, or I'll put a bullet

in your head.'

'Murphy!' Younger snapped.

The outlaw stared at Younger. 'Easy, Cole. Just let it play out.'

Mort, bruised and bloodied, staggered across to the safe and

within a few moments had it open. He turned and gave Murphy a

timid look.

The outlaw threw the sack at him. 'Start loading.'

While Mort stuffed that one, Murphy emptied the others and

tossed them at the teller.

Once they were filled, Mort stacked them on the counter. Murphy reached into the nearest one and took out a couple of bundles then put them inside his coat.

He gave Younger a sinister smile. 'See, nothing's changed.'

'We are all masters of our fate,' Cole responded.

Murphy smirked and walked out of the bank.

Frank and Younger walked over to stand near the door with the remaining money. Frank looked at Mort who was still a little stunned at it all.

'It wasn't meant to happen like this, Mort,' Frank said to him. He then turned to Younger. 'Don't like this, Cole.'

Younger tried to sound reassuring. 'When Pepper cuts loose, we'll have time to get to the horses. Before the smoke clears, we'll be half-way to Pine Ridge.'

'Action!'

Younger looked at Mort. 'That's your cue.'

The dazed teller opened the bank door and staggered outside. His arms were raised and Frank and Younger heard him blurt, 'They're robbing the bank! They're robbing the bank!'

No sooner had the words passed his lips when a shot rang out and Mort was shoved physically back through the opening.

Gulman could be heard shouting, 'Good! Good! Good!'

But it was far from good. The bloodstain high up on the left-side of Mort's shirt attested to that.

'Younger cursed under his breath as he knelt beside the fallen man.

Frank remained standing and looked down as his friend checked Mort's wound. He shook his head and muttered, 'Mort, I am sorry.'

'What happened?' Mort asked, still in shock.

'That skunk Murphy plugged you,' said Younger.

'And ruined my suit,' James added. Mort laughed at James' gallows humor.

Younger patted Mort on the shoulder. 'I don't think it's mortal, Mr. Goldstein. Maybe it's best if you sit this one out while we fix things.'

Mort nodded. 'Might I trouble you for a weapon? Just in case.'

Younger smiled at him. 'I don't think so, Mort. Can't have you shooting yourself in the foot with it. It would be right irresponsible.'

Mort nodded.

'One more thing. If I was you, I'd stick to bank tellering from now on. This acting caper can be quite dangerous.'

Once more, Younger patted him on the shoulder and stood up. He stared at Frank who said, 'I'm getting too old for this, Cole.'

'The game's afoot, old friend.'

'Watch out for Murphy.'

They headed out the door.

TWELVE

Once outside, Younger and Frank tossed the sacks to Old Joe and ran, as best they could, down the stairs, firing into the air.

Up on the ridge, overlooking town, Pepper reacted to his cue with all the actions of a sober man. He raised his rifle, sighted along the barrel, and fired.

Early that morning, before the sun had risen, Pepper had strategically placed two bundles of dynamite around town. The first to go was the newspaper office. The front of the building exploded in a shower of splinters.

Down below, Tilghman and the others came running from the jail, unaware that what was happening was real. They started to run towards the bank, while Frank and Cole Younger ran towards the haberdashery, firing in the air as they went.

Up until now, most of the people on the street thought that the activity was all part of the filming process.

But, all that changed when the second explosion rocked Fort Bowers.

Pepper worked the lever of his rifle and fired again. This time the courthouse exploded. He took particular pleasure in seeing it blown all to Hell. Then he hurried across to the cannon.

Pepper lit the fuse and turned away, plugging his ears with his fingers. The explosion rocked the very ground he stood on and a large orange flash spread across the ridge. When he turned back, the cannon was nothing more than a smoldering wreck.

When the courthouse went up, Tilghman, Masterson, and Bear stopped dead. This was all very wrong.

Tilghman glanced around himself at the chaos as it consumed the town. People were running for cover as debris rained down on the street. Above the background noise of yelling and screaming, Tilghman heard Gulman shouting, 'Cut! Cut! Cut!'

Selig burst from the jail, looking for Melody amid the confusion. He saw Becky and Mabel running for the general store, but there was no sign of Zoe or the children.

Murphy stood at the mouth of an alley, watching, waiting. Then he saw Tilghman and the others in the middle of the street and his mouth twisted up into a cruel smile.

He raised the rifle and fired.

Tilghman cursed bitterly. 'Damnnnn!'

He was unaware of the bullet which passed close to his head, its sound lost in the din. 'I see Zoe,' Masterson said.

'Where?'

'There, see?'

Tilghman saw his wife and made to move towards her when his way was blocked by the Joes, all mounted on horses, pointing guns at the three lawmen.

'What the hell is this?' Tilghman demanded.

'What do it look like?' Old Joe cackled. But there was no humor in his eyes. 'Back to the jail.'

'The hell I –'

The hammer went back on the old timer's gun. 'These ain't blanks no more, Marshal. They's the real thing. Not like that toy pistol you're holding.'

Resignedly, Tilghman tossed his gun on the ground as did Masterson and Bear. Then they turned and trudged back towards the jail under the watchful eye of Old Joe.

From a distance, Zoe Tilghman had seen it all.

Zoe rushed into Woody's gun shop to find Woody, Momma, Frankie, Tench and Malachi all there. There was movement behind her and Chuck appeared through the door.

'All hell's broke loose out there, Momma' Chuck moaned.

'That old man and his brood have put Bill in his own jail,' Zoe informed them. 'We have to do something.'

'What in blazes is happening?' Chuck snapped. 'It's crazy.'

'I'm not sure. But whatever it is, you can bet that lunatic Murphy's behind it.'

While they were talking, no one noticed Malachi and Tench take a six-gun and a Bowie knife from the cabinet behind the counter. They nodded at each other and slipped quietly out the back.

The door on the jail slammed shut behind the three lawmen and Masterson noticed Big Joe drop the keys into the pot-bellied stove. He looked to see whether Tilghman was taking notice.

Then the three Joes rummaged through drawers until they found what they wanted. Boxes of live ammunition.

Tilghman mumbled in disgust as the outlaws started to reload their weapons.

'How far do you think you'll get, Joe?' Tilghman asked the old man.

'Sorry, Bill, this ain't what I wanted. I been trying to find a way to stop all this, but it's gone too far down a bad man road. All I could think of was to comply and hope we all survive. Weird, but it's closest to the Good Book I could get right now. See, Murphy and his gang are just mean. Cole's a little crazy and this whole thing has kind of gotten … complicated.'

'Do what you got to do, Joe.

Where's Murphy?'

Old Joe shrugged. 'I don't rightly know.'

Outside, the main street was vacant, except for Murphy Jones and his henchmen. They stood in the middle of the street, looking around at the debris from the explosions that Pepper had set off.

Cherokee Waite said, 'Pepper sure got their attention. Our horses are tied out back. Let's get out of here.'

Arkansas Tom nodded in agreement. 'Give us our share, and we'll slap leather.'

Murphy shook his head. He was going nowhere. 'Hold on. Keep the streets clear for a few more minutes. I got some unfinished business.'

They all knew what he was talking about and didn't like the idea of hanging around long enough to satisfy Murphy's lust for revenge.

Billy Sunset asked, 'Why should we?'

'If you stick around, you can split my share.'

Ethics were one thing. Cash was another. They nodded. 'OK.'

Younger finished putting the tattered coat on and turned to face Frank. 'Does it say prospector?'

'It'll say shoot me, if we don't get out of here soon,' Frank growled.

Both had changed attire, and now wore something akin to rags.

'Well, get the saddlebags and we'll head to the livery.'

Frank stared at Cole for a moment. 'Why am I feeling Northfield creeping up my ass?'

Cole smirked, 'Frank, you worry too much."

Old Joe grimiced. 'We gotta be going, Marshal. Sorry to be leaving you cooped up like this, but … as I said … sorry.'

'

The old man gave him a wave and joined his sons as they headed out the back door.

He stopped dead, eyes wide. 'What in tarnation have you got there, woman?'

Old Joe had been expecting his wife to be there waiting with a wagon; not the horseless jalopy she now sat in, engine running.

Miss Darling smiled at him. 'Do you like it?'

'You can't drive one of these, Ma,' Little Joe declared.

'Just get your asses in here.'

'Do as your mama says, boys,' Old Joe ordered, 'get your asses into that contraption.'

Meanwhile, Cole and Frank had reached the livery where they found Melody and Russell in a heated discussion.

'You can't be that stupid! You were weeks away from being a free man. We could have had ...'

'Calm down, Missy,' Younger interrupted as they entered. 'Stupid? Goes without saying, but the fact is Mr. Russell here was ignorant of the plot.'

Frank said, 'If he hadn't been, perhaps he would have done a better job of holding our horses.'

'Well, this explosion went off and …well, they spooked and I …' Russell stammered.

Younger cut him off before he could say more. 'What's left in the livery?'

'One old mule and about fifty chickens.'

'Family reunion?' Younger said, referring to Russell's nickname. 'Well, Frank, not sure where this leaves us.'

'Up a creek,' Frank growled.

Younger nodded. 'Look, I'll just tell them I forced you to play along. My life won't change. And, so far, I'm not carrying any more lead. Believe me, I've had worse days.'

Younger forced the money he was holding into Russell's hands and said, 'Here, take this.'

'Where are the boys?' Zoe asked.

'They was here a minute ago,' Woody said, and then he noticed the missing knife and gun. 'Errrgh. Malachi and his knives. Damn it!'

'What?'

'They've taken a gun and knife from the cabinet.'

Zoe paled. 'Oh. No. You don't think they've gone to help Bill, do you?'

'Is the boy like his pa?'

'More than I'd like.'

'Then that's where they'll be.'

Starting towards the door, Zoe said, 'We have to find them.'

'Wait,' Woody snapped. He walked across to a gun cabinet and opened it. He took out three Winchesters and a couple boxes of cartridges. He passed one to Zoe and the other to Chuck. 'I got a feeling we'll need these.'

THIRTEEN

'Wish I had me a gun right now,' Masterson said. 'I feel a mite naked with Murphy running around out there somewhere.'

'You ain't the only one.'

'Look at that,' Bear said, pointing at the back door.

Tilghman watched the back door to the jail swing open and braced himself for what might happen next. What he wasn't prepared for was the arrival of Tench and Malachi as they ran through the opening.

The marshal breathed a sigh of relief. 'Boys, it's sure good to see you. Get us out of here.'

They looked around dumbly for the keys and Masterson said, 'In the stove.'

Tench opened the metal door and fished the ring of keys out and soon had the jail door unlocked.

'Get your weapons and make sure they're loaded,' Tilghman snapped and found his Colt and checked its loads.

Malachi said, 'We just saw that old man and his sons getting away.'

Tench nodded. 'Yeah. They were riding away in a car. It looked like that old lady was driving.'

'OK,' Tilghman acknowledged. 'You boys stay here.'

'No way, Pa.' Tench said and they started to run out the back door.

Zoe, Woody, and Chuck paused as they stepped out onto the boardwalk. They looked up and down the street. Everything seemed deserted.

'Too quiet,' Woody observed.

'I'll take quiet,' Zoe said. 'Let's go get Bill. He can help us find the boys.'

They stepped cautiously out into the debris-strewn street and started along it at a steady pace. Zoe stepped around a fallen camera and kept moving. Further along the street, a thin line of smoke rose into the air from the courthouse.

Once they reached the bank, a figure stumbled outside, a bloody patch on his shirt. All three of them swung their weapons in Mort's direction.

Mort held up his hands and winced as pain shot through him.

'Get back inside,' Chuck snapped.

'You got a spare one of those?' Mort asked, pointing at the gun in Chuck's hands.

'Can you shoot?'

'Quite proficiently.'

Chuck reached into his shirt and took out his M1911 and walked across to Mort. 'Just cock it and keep pulling the trigger.'

Mort nodded.

Chuck was about to continue with the others when he caught movement across the street. '*The freight office!*'

No sooner had the words escaped his lips when gunfire erupted. Arkansas Tom's first shot splintered the butt of the Winchester in Chuck's hands and the force of the blow spun him around.

Zoe ducked instinctively, rose again quickly, and fired back at the outlaw. Her shot hit him in the shoulder and a pained shout escaped his lips. Still he moved forward.

Woody fired three fast shots at the freight office and shattered the window. More gunfire exploded as the other outlaws opened fire.

'The wagon!' Woody shouted. 'Get behind it!'

They all ran for the wagon, leaving Mort standing by himself. Bullets zipped about him, chewing splinters from uprights and smashing a window behind him.

But Mort stood rock-steady under the incoming fire. Finally, he had had enough.

Arkansas Tom looked at his bleeding shoulder and reloaded, even as he favored the wound. He spotted Chuck and Zoe making their way to the jail, but he made a fatal error. He did not see Mordecai Goldstein.

Arkansas Tom's last motion was raising his gun towards the Tilghmans.

Mort did not hear the seven shot .45 fire seven times. Arkansas Tom never knew he was killed by a normally passive, lowly bankteller.

Mort dropped the pistol and walked into the Tilghman-Masterson Saloon. It had been a long day.

'Looks like your boy was quite the marksman, Chuck,' Woody pointed out as Mort disappeared into the saloon.

'Damn, didn't know he had that in him,' Chuck cursed out loud, drawing a stern look from Zoe.

Lead created furrows in the wagon's timber work while bullet strikes played a staccato tune as they hammered into it.

'I'm going to circle around and slip into the jail by the back door,' said Woody. 'You all be right here?'

Zoe rose and fired another shot. 'We'll be fine.'

Woody gave Chuck his rifle. 'Take this. I got a six-gun inside my coat.'

Then Woody broke cover and started for the narrow laneway beside the jail.

When he ducked into the alley he came upon Red, Boyd, and William, who were taking shelter there.

'What's going on, Johnny?' Red asked.

'They decided to rob the bank for real.'

'Anything we can do?' Boyd asked.

'Stay out of the way.'

The hurt caused by his words was written across each of their faces and Woody said, 'I tell you what. I had to leave my gun shop in a hurry. I think I left the door open. Can you fellers go down there and keep an eye on it for me?'

They smiled. 'Sure can.'

'Good.'

Woody left them to it and kept moving until he reached the back door of the jail and met the boys, Tench and Malachi coming out.

'Where do you think you two are going?'

Tilghman nodded grimly at Woody as he walked in through the door, a boy in each hand. He crooked his head towards the cell they'd just vacated, and Woody put them inside.

'Wait here,' he said, before closing the door.

'What's going on outside, Woody?' Tilghman asked.

'Murphy and the others have Zoe and Chuck pinned down.'

'Any sign of Younger?'

'Nope.'

'OK. Here's what we'll do. When we leave here, you go to the livery and see if they're there. Bat, you take Chuck and run the Joes down.. Bear and I will take care of Murphy and the others.'

They all nodded and followed Tilghman out the door.

Once outside they fanned out. Woody broke left to head for the livery, while Bat signaled to get Chuck's attention. Chuck and Zoe were under steady fire at the wagon and missed the wild gesticulations of the deputy behind them. Trying again, this time Bat gave a quick whistle and Chuck turned to see what was going on.

The gunfire from the freight office continued as he told Zoe that he was needed elsewhere and for her to keep her head down.

Tilghman brought up his Colt and, as cool as ever, blew off all six shots while he walked towards Zoe's position.

'Are the boys OK?' she asked desperately.

'They're fine.'

'Thank God. What are we going to do now, Sheriff?' Zoe questioned.

When Woody arrived at the livery he found Younger, Frank James, Russell, and Melody standing together with the 'Chicken Man' holding the loot.

He crept in behind them and said, 'Go easy now. I like your travel clothes, gentlemen. Step away, Miss Melody.'

Melody started to move toward Woody. Her expression pleaded with the gunsmith for Russell. 'But he didn't know anything about this.'

'Same with Frank. I didn't give him a choice,' Younger added.

'Not for me to determine. Now, Mr. Younger and Mr. James just turn away and keep your hands in sight,' the gunsmith directed.

Once they had complied, Woody snapped, 'Start walking.'

William, Red, and Boyd made their way to Woody's gunshop. Bobbing and weaving like three old boxers.

Red was the last to slide in the door and observed William grabbing one of Woody's shotguns, 'What do you think you are doing?'

'I'm getting me a gun,' William growled. 'What does it look like?'

William took the sawn-off shotgun from the rack and found a box of shells. Then he started to hobble towards the open door.

'Where are you going now, you old fool?' Boyd groaned, not wanting to hear the answer.

William stopped and stared at his friend. 'I figure I ain't got long for this here world. I'm thinking I might as well shoot someone while I still can.'

'Good grief,' Red moaned.

Boyd looked at him. 'Can you believe this?'

'Here comes a couple of them now, boys!' William shouted from out on the boardwalk.

The two men hurried outside and were just in time to see William unload both barrels at the riders who were thundering along the street.

The shotgun's roar rolled along the main street and a large, hand-painted sign above the general store disintegrated under the double charge.

'Dagnabit! I missed!' Bill cursed out loud as he tried to reload.

Boyd vocalized, 'That surprise you? You blind, old coot.'

Red stepped forward and wrenched the gun from his friend's hands.

"Gotta say you still got gumption, old friend. You're stupid as dirt and blind as a bat, but gumption you got!"

William stared at him indignantly. 'Red. What you go and do that for?'

'You old fool,' Red snapped. 'That was Bat Masterson and Chuck Tilghman you tried to shoot!'

Red rubbed at his temples and shook his head. ' Boyd, get him under control before I shoot him myself.'

Tilghman ducked back down as a slug passed close and another slammed into the side of the wagon. He slipped fresh rounds into the Colt and was about to rise and fire again when movement across the street caught his eye.

A wounded Billy Sunset had shifted position and now had a clear field of fire at them from an alley between two buildings. He raised his weapon and sighted on Zoe.

'Zoe! No!'

Tilghman could do nothing.

Two gunshots rang out close together and because Tilghman had his eyes closed awaiting the terrible moment his wife was killed, he sensed rather than saw that Zoe was still alive.

Tilghman opened his eyes in time to see Sunset fall forward and his weapon drop from his fist.

Behind him was Cole Younger, a smoking six-gun in his hand that Woody had missed.

Younger then reached down and touched at his right side. He brought his hand away and it was red with blood. He gave a wry smile. 'Well, hell, what's one more?'

Then he too, fell forward.

Behind him stood Woody, still clutching his six-gun, a faint wisp of smoke trailing from the barrel.

Tilghman shook his head as another ricochet buzzed past his ear. 'I've had enough of this.'

'Bill, what are you doing?' Zoe shouted at her husband.

He ignored her and stood up then walked out into the open. He raised his gun and started to fire at Murphy Jones who was hunkered down behind a trough. The outlaw saw him coming and rose to meet the challenge.

Two hard men walking toward each other firing their weapons.

Trying to take advantage of the situation, Cherokee Waite emerged and trained his gun on Tilghman.

Before he could fire, however, Zoe and Bear cut loose with a fusillade of shots that had the outlaw doing a macabre dance with each impact until he, too, fell to the ground.

By some bizarre circumstance, Tilghman's gun locked back, signaling his weapon was empty at the same time as Murphy's hammer fell on a spent round.

Tilghman cursed and threw his gun away, as did Murphy. The latter gave a cruel smile. 'Ahh, the sweet smell of revenge. Right, Bill?'

The two men hit head on like twin locomotives without freight cars. Murphy swung a wild punch at Tilghman's head which the marshal blocked easily with his left arm and with his right fist, drove a solid blow into the snarling outlaw's face.

Murphy staggered back, and blood began to flow from the corner of his mouth. He wiped at it and grinned.

'Still life in the old man yet, huh?' he sneered.

'More than you can handle,' Tilghman countered and closed the distance between them again.

He walked into a straight left and a right cross that seemed to set him back on his heels. The coppery taste of blood flooded Tilghman's mouth and he spit in the dirt at his feet.

The two men closed for battle again, trading savage blows.

Across the street, Frank James bent down and picked up the gun that Younger had used on Billy Sunset. He cocked it and the barrel wavered as he tried to get a bead on Murphy.

A hand clamped over the hammer, so the weapon couldn't fire. Woody said, 'Don't go trying to shoot that far, Frank, when you can't see your boots.'

'I can see fine enough to shoot Murphy.'

Air whooshed from Tilghman's lungs as Murphy went low with a hard punch to his middle. The marshal gritted his teeth and backed away.

By now both men were sucking in great gulps of air.

Murphy stepped in close and swung again. Tilghman was starting to slow and the blow crashed against his chin, dropping him to his knees. Murphy brought up his own knee and it crunched into Tilghman's jaw.

The marshal flopped onto his back, his eyes rolling back in his head. Murphy stepped in and kicked him in the side.

Tilghman felt as though he'd been kicked by a mule and thought that a rib had broken. He bit back a cry of pain and tried to roll away from the next one which struck home as well.

Pain ripped through the lawman's body and he felt paralyzed, unable to move, vulnerable.

Murphy glanced about and found what he wanted. He staggered across to a large piece of timber on the ground. He scooped it up and turned around.

Tilghman had managed to drag himself from the ground and hit the outlaw with a shoulder to his middle.

The air rushed from Murphy's lungs and the two men crashed through an old hitch rail and onto the boardwalk outside The Powder Keg Saloon.

Both men fell hard. Murphy let out a cry of pain when his back hit the rail hard. They rolled apart and seemed to lay there for a drawn-out moment before again struggling to their feet.

Murphy still showed the effects of the impact with the boardwalk and took a little time to find his balance. The bleeding Tilghman, however, was a little quicker to recover despite his broken rib and rushed at the outlaw, wrapping his arms around him and drove him backward.

With a shattering crash the pair broke through the large front window of The Powder Keg. Glass rained down around them as they hit the floor inside, scattering the tables and chairs about them.

Tilghman felt the burn of tiny cuts as the glass slivers showered most of his exposed skin. Beneath him, Murphy hissed a curse and fought to roll the lawman from on top.

Raising up, Tilghman punched the outlaw in the face. Once, twice. Each time, Murphy grunted.

The Fort Bowers' marshal climbed tiredly to his feet and grabbed a handful of Murphy's hair. He dragged the outlaw to his feet and punched him in the mouth.

Murphy slammed up against the bar, the edge of the polished counter adding to his discomfort. Tilghman spit out a globule of blood and bent down. He grasped the outlaw's legs and with all his strength, heaved him backward over the bar.

As Murphy's legs flipped over they caught the shelves behind it. Bottles and glasses were brought down with a cataclysmic smash and glass, along with alcohol, showered the downed man.

Tilghman leaned against the bar, drawing in large breaths. Beside him was a half-full bottle of whiskey and he seized it with a trembling hand. He lifted it to his lips and took a long pull.

The liquid burned all the way down and he splashed some of it on his face and felt the sting of the many cuts and scrapes.

The marshal leaned over the bar and stared down at the moaning form of Murphy. He turned the bottle up and poured the rest of the whiskey over the outlaw. The glass-covered man coughed and spluttered.

'Get up, Mr. Jones.' Tilghman growled. 'Time for you to go back to prison.'

There was the crunch of broken glass behind Tilghman and he turned to see Bear stepping through the shattered window. In his right hand was Tilghman's discarded Colt, in his left was his own weapon.

'Just come to see if you were still alive,' Bear said to the weary marshal.

'I'll live.'

Bear handed him the weapon. 'Careful, it's loaded.'

'The others?'

'Dead.'

Tilghman nodded and wiped at his bloody mouth. 'I'm way too old for this shit.'

Suddenly Bear's eyes widened. '*Look out!*'

Tilghman turned to see that Murphy had risen to his feet behind the bar. In his hands was a sawn-off shotgun kept under the counter by the barkeep. He brought it up, hammers thumbed back.

It was just coming level when Tilghman's handgun spat fire. Two .45 slugs slammed into Murphy's chest in quick succession. Twin small, red-tainted explosions erupted from the killer's chest and he was punched back once more into the wall behind the bar that had previously held the shelves.

The shotgun kept rising and discharged into the ceiling. Debris fell like rain and the spent shotgun clattered to the floor, the report still ringing in Tilghman's ears.

With his gun raised he edged forward and peered over the bar and looked down at the mortally-wounded Murphy.

'Why did you try it, Murphy? You had no chance.'

The killer coughed as blood rose in his throat. He swallowed and said, 'Needed to be free, Marshal. Kill you. You kill me. Either way I'm free.'

Tilghman shook his head. 'Damnation.'

'Old Joe says maybe … maybe not.'

Murphy gave a wan smile and died.

There was a flurry of movement behind the two lawmen and they turned to see Zoe framed by the broken window. Tilghman nodded to his wife. 'It's over.'

FOURTEEN

Tilghman sat on the steps outside The Powder Keg, Zoe tending his various cuts and scrapes, when Woody pulled up in a buckboard. In the back was the wounded Cole Younger, beside him, his longtime friend, Frank James.

Younger opened his eyes, his face a pasty gray color. 'For the record, let's say Frank had nothing to do with this,' he winced as a wave of pain swept through him. 'This one bit me pretty hard.'

Tilghman nodded. 'I saw what you did, Cole. I won't forget it.'

Frank said, 'Yet another Cole Younger tale.'

Cole coughed. 'Full of sound and fury... Signifying nothing.'

'Let's get him over to the doc.'

Tilghman looked at Woody. 'You might want to let them boys out of jail while you're at it.'

'I figured on leaving them there until suppertime. Might make them think twice about doing fool things.'

The lawman nodded. 'Might at that.'

The buckboard rattled away and Tilghman glanced around the street.

He saw Mabel helping the wounded, but animated Mort out of the saloon. He was telling the operator about his harrowing experience. Somehow, he seemed taller than before.

Then the marshal saw Red, Boyd, and William. They were now seated outside of the hotel. He heard William growl, 'I can't believe you took my gun away. I'd have stopped them outlaws.'

'More like to have killed one of us, you old fool,' Boyd told him.

William scowled at his friend and was about to keep the argument going when Red patted him on the shoulder. 'Come on, Billy Bonney, I'll take you over to the Tilghman-Masterson Saloon and buy you a drink.'

'What about me?' Boyd asked.

'Get your own. You were the one who let him have the gun in the first place.'

The marshal smiled.

Selig, Melody and Russell emerged from the hotel. All three were smiling. From the look of Selig, he'd come to accept Russell.

Tilghman frowned as he saw Miss Hathaway skulking around a water barrel. He watched interestedly as she removed its lid and Gulman's head appeared above the rim.

'Would you get a look at that,' Bear said, bemused.

Tilghman looked along the street and saw Chuck riding along, towing the car the Joes had stolen. Behind the wheel was Masterson.

They stopped where the marshal and Zoe sat, and Chuck gave his father a wry smile. 'Well ... They must have run out of gas.'

Tilghman smirked, 'And gotten away on foot?'

Masterson held up a bag of money.

'Hard to believe they left that behind,' Tilghman noted.

'Yeah, it's a mystery,' Masterson agreed. 'They really weren't true bad men, Marshal.'

'Yep, figure they'll go straight, Pa.'

'You just let 'em go?' Tilghman quizzed.

Chuck replied, 'No, they just sorta slipped away.'

Tilghman gave them both a knowing look. 'Uh huh.'

'Good Lord, Bill,' Zoe gasped. 'Is that who I think it is?'

Tilghman's gaze shifted to the other end of the street where Pepper had staggered into view, clothes tattered and scorch marks all over, his hair singed.

Behind him rode two men, both hunched in the saddle, tired after hard riding. Bass Reeves and Wyatt Earp.

Tilghman chuckled. 'Late as usual.'

They halted in the middle of the street.

Wyatt asked, 'Bill, you know this character?'

'Fool, damn near killed his self,' Bass grumbled.

'Yeah, I know him.'

'So, do I,' snapped Zoe, and before anyone could move, she came to her feet and quickly crossed to the three men, then let fly with a right fist which rocked Pepper back onto his heels. Then his eyes rolled back and he collapsed to the street.

Zoe wheeled around to find Tilghman staring at her.

'What?' she demanded.

Saying nothing, Tilghman just smiled.

1 year later

Outside the show tent at the other end of the alley, a large placard read: *"Relive the Wild West: featuring The Infamous Cole Younger and Frank James in the full-length film, "Bill Tilghman and the Passing of the Outlaws"."*

On a bench seat placed on the boardwalk at the mouth of the alley, sat three old men.

'Been thinking,' Red said.

'Yeah? Well don't hurt yourself,' William grumbled.

'Moving Pictures could be the future.'

Boyd shook his head. 'Nah, just a passing fad, friends, just a passing fad.'

-

After Bill Tilghman's death, Bat Masterson was asked about his friend's life. He spoke slowly and, through tears, said, "Bill Tilghman was the greatest of us all."

SCREENWRITER'S NOTES:

Although "Bill Tilghman and the Outlaws" is a work of historical fiction, it has at its core a true event.

In 1915, Bill Tilghman, Oklahoma lawman (July 4, 1854 – November 1, 1924), decided to make what we now call a reality show. In this case, a reality-based motion picture show.

He made a full-length flicker, using himself as the lead, tracking and arresting some real-life, but mostly not very famous, outlaws. Eight minutes of this film still exist and can be found on YouTube.

A short article about that film in True West magazine sparked in me the musing; if I was an outlaw in the film, I wouldn't cotton to Tilghman arresting me for pretend, making a fool of me for all to see. Nope, I would want revenge.

From there my imagination took over.

As my "let's rob the bank for real" idea came to germination, I began to consider one more thing; a chance to right what I considered to be an historical wrong.

In 1924 at the age of 69, while still working as a lawman, Bill Tilghman was murdered by a low-down coward. Unfortunately, for some reason that's the predominant thing most people know about Bill Tilghman. The way he died.

I wanted to create a story that mythologized Tilghman. Maybe in some small way to put him on the same pedestal as world famous Old West lawmen, like Bat Masterson and Wyatt Earp. Could I right part of the wrong done to his reputation?

While I was at it, I also added the true life legendary African American sheriff, Bass Reeves to the story because he too should be better known by western history buffs.

Putting these four lawmen in the same town in the making of a movie is pure fiction, but Earp and Masterson where involved in early picture making as, of course, was the aforementioned Tilghman.

Bass Reeves on the other hand, was not often depicted on film because, I think, of his race. To me, it's ironic that once again Reeves was cut from film. This time he was cut from ours. Not because of racism, but because the story arc didn't fit .But I was able to restore his story arc to our book.

To see Reeves arrest of the real life Brunter Brothers on film, look for our short on Amazon Prime, "Tales of the Wild West," Episode 7, "Bass Reeves and the Brunter Brothers," starring Grammy nominee, Guy Davis, as well as Richard Cutting, who plays Murphy in our Tilghman film.

Among the book's true life characters are Zoe Tilghman, who was Bill's second wife. His first wife either died or left him. History is unclear. The much younger Zoe was the love of his life and by all accounts she adored him.

The Tilghman children's names are real, but all of the depictions are fictional.

The other real-life people depicted in our story include :

➢ Cole Younger,

➢ Frank James,

➢ Libby "Alice" Thompson, Sweetwater, Texas, who died at the age of 98,

- Arkansas Tom (who had a role in the original "Bill Tilghman and the Passing of the Outlaws"),and later was killed while robbing a bank,
- William Selig, a film pioneer, credited with helping popularize Tom Mix, Fatty Arbuckle, and Bronco Billy Anderson among others.

The reader may also recognize some Western film actor names used in the book, like William, Boyd, and Red. William Boyd was the actor who played Hopalong Cassidy in over 100 films and even more T.V. episodes. One of Cassidy's sidekicks was a character named Red.

John Russell was star of one of T.V.'s great 30-minute Westerns, "Lawman" and many other Western films, including Clint Eastwood's "Pale Rider" and "The Outlaw Josie Wales" and John Wayne's "Rio Bravo."

The character, Woody Jefferies salutes two black film stars, Woody Strode, star of John Ford's "Sargent Rutledge" and "The

Professionals" and Herb Jeffries, the first African American singing cowboy, who starred in four features that played almost exclusively to black audiences.

Murphy Jones is a play on a favorite T.V. series of my teenage years, "Alias Smith and Jones," starring Ben Murphy and Peter Duel, later Roger Davis.

Finally, this is not a pure novelization.

Ben Bridges began working on the novel, but couldn't finish the project due to scheduling conflicts. The talented Brent Towns stepped in and did the majority of the writing. Then my wife, Eydie and I edited and re-edited to match the book and film's tonality. Curiously, the book's ending differs wildly from the movie. I think the version used in the book is better for the book and the version used in the film, which was devised by Stuntman Jeff Wilhelm and Director Wayne Shipley with input from yours truly, works better in the film. But, judge for yourself.

Lastly, be sure to check out the original music written for "Bill Tilghman and the Outlaws" by the Walker Avenue Gang on YouTube, itunes, CDBaby, Spotify and Amazon. I especially recommend "Melody" the love song referenced in the novelization, as well as "Bad Man Road" and "Hell's Train" both also hinted at in our book.

And, of course, be sure to see the movie!

THANK YOU FOR READING!

If you enjoyed this book, we would appreciate your customer review on your book seller's website or on Goodreads.

Also, we would like for you to know that you can find more great books like this one at www.CreativeTexts.com

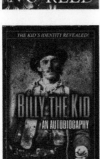

CPSIA information can be obtained
at www.ICGtesting.com
Printed in the USA
BVHW071433110219
539954BV00005B/470/P